Jessa's Prayer

Carolyn Moor

Copyright © 2003 Carolyn Moor
All rights reserved.

ISBN 1-59109-574-3

Jessa's Prayer

TABLE OF CONTENTS

1. Decision ... 1
2. First Steps ... 11
3. Meeting Ian ... 19
4. Landslide! ... 41
5. Fuller Lodge ... 43
6. The News ... 55
7. In-House Call ... 61
8. A Different Kind Of Dream ... 67
9. Clarity ... 75
10. "No Estan En Casa" ... 83
11. "Thanks Dad" ... 87
12. A Little Info ... 93
13. "We Are Looking For Jessica Franklin" ... 103
14. Snowfall ... 107
15. Bozeman, Montana ... 115
16. Alive! ... 119
17. Adventist Fire ... 123
18. What's With Bozeman? ... 137
19. Are You Ready Mrs. Franklin? ... 139
20. No Flight Pattern ... 145
21. Crossing The Dateline ... 151
22. Don't Go In There! ... 155
23. Keeping Secret ... 163
24. Standoff ... 171
25. A Soldier's Generosity ... 179
26. Goodbye, Bozeman ... 191
27. The End Before The Beginning (One Year Later) ... 201

CHAPTER ONE

DECISION

"Look!" She thought to herself. "Here they come again! Is it the same flock as before? Or is it a different bunch of small black birds darting about like crazy? The way this wind is throwing things around I wonder how the poor things don't crash." She looked up at him, stating "Chores are done, and it is getting late. We should call it a day. I'm heading in and you had better get back while it is still safe, and thank you again Ian, mending that fence alone would have taken me all night, and it would not have been this strong! I am thankful to have you as my neighbor."

As he looked down at her his strong face softened. His brown, green-flecked eyes twinkled amid black waves of wind tossed hair and he spoke in a low tone Jessa had never heard Ian use before. "I would be thankful to be a closer neighbor, Jessa." And with that he took a step closer, caught from the wind a lock of her long dark hair, lifted it to his lips and pressed it there. Closing his eyes, Ian breathed in slowly and deeply. Upon opening them again he read her own, sky blue 'mirrors of the soul' and saw the fear, shock and disbelief there.

Dropping the lock and stepping back again, he quipped, "Forgive me Mrs. Franklin, if that is all you need then I will be on my way." He spun away from her while calling for his dog and strode across the wooden bridge to the far side of the river to swing a lanky leg over his motorcycle.

Jessa watched as Ian kick-started the bike and could smell

the thin puff of blue exhaust it left behind on the chill evening air as he sped away along the trail and into the forest.

Stunned and breathless, her heart pounding, Jessa watched as Ian faded into the darkness of the tree line. She could not believe what had happened just now, for the man had hardly spoken to her in all these years and now this! "Does this mean he believes that Grant is dead?" Her voice quavered, and a tear started to form as the thought pierced her heart. Feeling so alone she simply could not stand it anymore, Jessa cried aloud to the earliest of the stars, "It's been so long Grant, <u>WHERE ARE YOU?</u>"

But the stars held no answers.

Feeling a familiar licking at her hand helped Jessa to snap out of her misery enough to pick up the lantern and turn towards the cabin with the big dog at her side. Her constant companion and guardian was Big Blue Bozeman, a huge and hairy, bounding, and to her at least, a beautiful friend.

Bozeman had one blue eye and an inquisitive nature that often made him look as if he understood her better than what a dog should, especially when his ears were up, listening intently. The dog had been a gift from her husband three years ago when just a pup, and at times when Grant would leave on another mission she could not help but wonder if the gift was not actually a consolation prize for his chronic absence.

Jessa had married her high school sweetheart six years ago after his graduation from college. It was a beautiful outdoor June wedding in their home state of Montana, with all of their family and friends in attendance. "It seems a lifetime ago," she thought to herself "and a world away."

They reached the porch now, the woman and the dog. She pulled off her boots as she opened the door for him, and Bozeman entered readily to trot straight to the small woodstove in the middle of the room and lie on his mat there. Jessa set the lantern inside and brought in an armload of wood to keep the fire burning into the night, and then with a foot she shut the door against the cold wind. Stepping over to the stove she dropped her load into the wood box, then returned to the door to bolt it for the night.

Jessa patted Bozeman and had him move aside so she could stoke the smoldering fire and add more wood, then closed the small door and moved to the kitchen to soon return with her teapot full of fresh water for heating. With that done she headed to her bedroom to change into her sweat pants and shirt. Returning to her kitchen with the dirty clothes of the day she set to washing them in the sink, which she did by way of the only indoor pump. After wringing out the water as best she could, Jessa hung them on the clothesline that stretched from one end of the kitchen to the other and then proceeded to take her nightly spit bath with the washcloth, bar of soap, and of course, cold water. After having wrapped her sopping wet hair in a large towel, Jessa proceeded to wash out the body cloth then hung it to dry next to her jeans.

As she reached down a mug from a cupboard for her tea she noted once again how bare the shelves looked. Almost out of her herbals, too. Still a little beans and rice though and there were two more pumpkins in the garden that had also supplied many quarts of canned vegetables, once she had finally figured out how to process them on top of her woodstove, luckily without too much disaster! "Humph. Two more pumpkins!" Her face winced as she thought aloud, for Jessa was sick of pumpkin. Sick of beans and rice for that matter, but those were all that was left aside from a few old canned goods items. Was it enough to feed herself for a few more weeks? By then the snows would keep her home.

That was it then. She had to go to town for the winter supplies. It would be the first time without Grant. They had always done that together, before his disappearance.

Jessa's husband was part of an elite team of seismologists, geologists and volcanologists, the only people on the planet capable of accurately predicting the time and place of an earthquake, volcanic eruption or tsunami. In the last three years of their marriage he had been gone nearly as much as at home, but at least he was faithful in writing to her twice a week and calling to relay messages as often, no matter what country he had been called away to. But now, this time, the communiqués had stopped trickling in. At first it was obviously because he was so intensely busy and the situation was unstable for several reasons.

The first reason would be the country: China. The government fiercely resented having to call in a team of outsiders. They resented having anything to do with other countries except conquering them. Coupled with the fact that their economy was in an uproar the government would really rather the rest of the world not have any inkling of how bad things had gotten. Part was due to the government's inefficiencies, and part to the terrible, freak weather that was causing flooding over thousands of miles of territories along the Yangtze and adjoining rivers. People were being washed away. Cities were under water causing disease to run rampant. The government did not want any sign of weakness to leak out and so to counter any 'rumors', its leaders were holding media conferences stating how in spite of some ill press their country's economy was thriving.

They struggled to 'save face' as is their way, honor could not be preserved if it were known how the government had allowed, even encouraged logging along the riverbanks to pad its own pockets, thus causing premature mudslides and breaks in the dikes.

Grant had also intimated to his wife that this particular region was unstable even for his team. "Better not expect me until you see the whites of my eyes" he had said while trying to smile before kissing her goodbye that day. That was two months ago.

"It has been nearly three weeks since his last letter, and longer since hearing his voice." She mused, "The longest three weeks imaginable!"

Now the time had come to venture out for supplies, and information.

At first, being all alone in the wild, just the two of them in their Canadian wilderness home, seemed so romantic to the newlyweds. Like Adam and Eve in the garden, though they worked hard at building a home for themselves.

They had built their cabin while living out of a canvas tent and sleeping on the ground seemed so cozy, all wrapped up in their one sleeping bag. They would wake up smiling and work as one body with one objective, sharing their life. Only occasionally would they need outside help, and then Grant would hire Ian Fuller to help them lift the beams, or dig holes for posts. Jessa was strong for a woman, and Grant kept fit. They lived a clean healthy lifestyle and so were an efficient team.

Fuller had worked hard nearly everyday of his life on his family's fifth generation ranch and farm. He was taller and more muscular than Grant, and could out lift the both of them.

Sitting on her couch now and thinking of the times the three of them would be working together, and how Grant would keep them lighthearted with his quick wit and sheer energy, Jessa felt the joy of those days coming back to her. It had puzzled her though that Ian would rarely look directly into her eyes or speak directly to her. Even in her presence he spoke to her through her husband, "How are you and your wife today, Grant?" Which made her feel like a 'less than'. Over time though she came to know him a little better and learned about his respectful upbringing, and that this was what he was showing her by not trying to get more familiar. She belonged to Grant and Ian showed respect for that. That was one thing of many she would be taught about respect by the Fuller family.

And this was why it bothered her so much that Ian had slipped up today. "It has to mean that in his mind Grant simply is not coming back, for whatever reason." She could not blame Ian, for her own mind had been nagging her with such thoughts, 'what if' scenarios such as "Perhaps he has met someone more exciting than simple little me?" or "What if I am not enough for him anymore? After all, he has an important job and can write his own ticket these days, and as they say 'Power corrupts...'"

But somehow, she could not believe he could up and leave her without an explanation and yes, even an apology.

"Stay home this time..." He had said. "You will be safer here." He had said. Be safer from what? Be safer how? Home alone with no one but a dog for comfort? Jessa trusted that

Bozeman would fight a pack of hungry wolves for her, or a bear even, but he could not set a broken bone or stitch a bloody wound if need be, and she remembered the two hapless hunters who had luckily stumbled upon her cabin last week. One was still bleeding from the steel trap set by the neighbor to the south, whose land they had mistakenly been on. That neighbor only lived there for part of the year and was not home when the strangers broke-in, looking for help. Fortunately for them, when they stumbled onto the Franklin property Jessa was willing and able to help (though Bozeman uncharacteristically growled his disapproval at the two haggard men from his ordered position in the doorway.) Jessa had opened her medical kit and proceeded to swab, bandage and stitch the wailing man's foot, then the three of them rode her four wheeled motorcycle to Fuller lodge, with the disgruntled dog trotting closely behind, not once being distracted away from the trail by another animal's scent. Jessa had picked her way especially carefully over the bumpy trail, so as not to jostle the injured man on the seat behind her. She was so intent on this that there was no chance of her noticing the movements of the other man riding on the back rack of the quad. She had no clue anyone would want to attach an electronic tracking device to her vehicle.

The ranch foreman drove them in his pickup the last four miles to town with Jessa and the wounded man riding next to him, with the taller man and Bozeman riding in the back, each staring at the other in mistrust.

While in town, and after seeing to the care of the wounded man, Jessa had checked for any messages from her husband, but there were none. And so despondently, she thanked the postmaster and trading post owner, Ignacious, and returned to Frank who waited patiently with Bozeman at the truck. Later, while motoring homeward bound, Jessa wondered why she had not detained Frank for an hour longer so that she could use his truck to haul supplies back to her waiting quad at the ranch, then realized it all seemed so useless at the time; that is, living. It was then she realized that she had a problem.

Being rid of the suspicious strangers, Bozeman could now

enjoy bounding along behind, now checking out the many other animal scents along the trail to their home.

Jessa hungered for conversation. Sometimes her mind would play tricks on her and strike up conversations in her head, simply to pass the time of course. Usually it was nothing of a serious note, merely a bit of friendly chatter to add flavor to an otherwise all too quiet existence. But one day when she was gathering eggs in the henhouse (and the chickens were worse than her dog for company), she could have sworn she heard a female voice, rather old and cackling, saying, "Dearie, why don't you try over here first? I do lay the very <u>best</u>, you know!" Jessa remembered how she had jumped and gasped that day! That was the day she had saddled old Rory and headed out to the Fuller's settlement, for there would be people there, not talking chickens.

Jessa remembered being in town that first year when Grant introduced her to Mr. and Mrs. Fuller. They were in their old pickup truck outside the feed store, and though they were polite enough they seemed distant somehow, rather like their only surviving son, Ian. Well, not so distant after a few more chance encounters at least, and Jessa was grateful that in her times of solitude she had a place to visit if need be. After all, she had to traverse a small portion of their twenty seven thousand acres to get to town, as well as the other neighbors on this southern end must, but especially to the post office to check for a letter from Grant.

Sometimes Ian would ride chaperone. He had said his mother wanted it that way. "For Jessa's protection." And at the time she had no reason to doubt his word and was grateful for the company, conversation (although limited from him) and yes, the protection. She thought of the scene earlier today and touched her hair the way he had. Her body had forgotten all about breathing just then.

Jessa sat sipping her tea and contemplating. So much was different now. Things were changing the way the wind was changing the season. It was a time for making decisions.

She got up to put a chunk of wood in the stove and closed

its door, then tightened down the damper so it would burn more slowly and long. She patted Bozeman who rolled over for a tummy scratching. With that done she picked up the lantern and unbolted the door to head to the outhouse, with Bozeman leading the way for he knew her habits sometimes better than she did herself. After returning to the cabin and bolting the door Jessa washed her hands from the pump, then snatched up her hairbrush to set to the task of untangling the mass of still damp hair that had been blown about so furiously most of the day.

Sitting in the rocker she brushed and sang to Bozeman so that he would 'sing' back. They did this until her hair finally looked smoother than his, and her ears hurt from his howls and barks. In days gone by they would sometimes wrestle for fun and exercise, but when the dog reached her own weight of one hundred thirty pounds, it was time to stop.

Bozeman settled down now and went to sleep. His mistress planned to do the same as soon as her head would let her. She wandered back to the kitchen and threw open every cupboard. Bare, empty, hollow, the words came to her. She was tired of staying hungry in order to make the supplies last or because she had already eaten what was appetizing, and what was left, well it was not appealing. There were two more cans and a couple of packages besides the beans and rice. There had been a garden but the summer had ended rather abruptly and only the squashes remained. Ugh. How long had it been since she'd had fresh fruit? The tender young apple and pear trees they had planted barely survived the last winter, and had not produced much yet, only a token promise of the good things to come. There was also the small greenhouse they kept warm with smudge pots that had a few young tomato plants, but they were doing about as well as the fruit trees. She wanted variety. She wanted to feel satisfied after a meal. It was good fertile land if you knew how to respect it, and every time Grant left she respected the land like crazy. Never would she go anywhere without Big Blue Bozeman by her side.

Boze had learned early that he was Jessa's dog and he took

great pride in that capacity, always either by her side or within earshot of her soft voice. He could tell instantly by the sound of her voice if she needed his protection, she did not need to shout. Only once had she ever been sorry about that, the time he 'saved' her from the skunk, unfortunately for him. She watched him sleeping. He was dreaming, she knew from the twitching legs it was another chase dream.

Jessa wished she could dream of chasing rabbits or foxes instead of what she had been going through these past couple of weeks. Watching Boze, she thought of those happy times before Grant became so immersed in his work. Had he wanted her to love this dog in place of a baby? Perhaps, and it's a good thing, she thought, that they had not as yet anyway brought a child into this world, as Grant would not be around much to be a part of their baby's growth. Still, things would not be so lonely around here.

"GRRR..." Bozeman jumped up growling, his ears lifted, listening. Jessa got the rifle down from its rack on the wall and checked it, yes, the safety was on, and carefully unbolted and opened the door. The lantern light spilled out into the night no faster than did her 'Bozeman dog'. The chickens were flapping about and cackling wildly.

"At least not in a woman's voice!" Jessa felt oddly relieved and had to smile at herself in spite of the impending carnage.

Bozeman had streaked off toward the sound and a fight ensued, the lean coyote having thought these penned fowl to be easy prey was getting his lesson in manners. He yelped once, thus dropping the struggling hen from his mouth and suddenly realizing an urgent appointment elsewhere, he leaped back over the high wire mesh fence to race away zigzagging through the brushy steep slope of the southwest ridge.

The poor frazzled hen cackled disapprovingly after the wild thing then shook out her feathers until some fell away and strode with her ruffled dignity up the ramp of her house and back to her bed.

"Thank you Big Blue Bozeman!" Jessa smiled and bowed royally at her dog as he came bounding back onto the porch.

He was all excited of course and wanted more of that varmint, but that would have meant leaving his home unprotected and he just didn't do that, for he was <u>not</u> a wild thing. Together they returned to the henhouse and closed the forgotten door.

"Well boy, shall we turn in now?" Jessa yawned while placing the rifle back on the wall. It had been a long day, although less lonely what with Ian helping out and all. 'He is a good neighbor,' she thought, 'and that is how it must stay.' Sighing, she bolted the door before turning down the lantern and went to bed.

CHAPTER TWO

FIRST STEPS

As the sun's rays peeked through the curtain and edged along her face then under an eyelash to invade her dreams of Grant, whitewashing them away, Jessa felt unbearable separation and longing for him as she awoke, and her decision became written, as if it were in stone, that she would find him no matter what the cost, or the outcome.

Jessa knew she could not stay home much longer without a trek to town, as she had already waited past the usual date for storing up the winter supplies. They had always done that together, she and Grant, until now.

She'd had enough to tide her over because she was alone, and so the food lasted longer, but there were other things such as white gas for the lantern, a bottle of shampoo would be nice, ammunition a must, toothpaste and feminine hygiene products, some new leather gloves and jeans and clothing in general that simply wear out. They would need flour, salt and sugar, fresh fruit would be especially scrumptious for the wild strawberries and plums were gone as well as the blackberries.

But those things could wait, if indeed they even mattered anymore. She had to find Grant first before she would know. "Has he left me forever? Was I not the wife he wanted after all? Wouldn't he be here if I were?" Those same thoughts kept returning to wear away her spirit.

Her decision having been made, Jessa became a woman of action, "Bozeman, you and I are _out_ of here so let's get with it!"

Instantly the big dog was on his feet and excitedly jumping about. He had heard her excitement and knew they were headed outside and some-where! He watched his mistress now as she took down the rifle and checked the safety. Hunting! They were going hunting! "Woof!" Bozeman jumped and circled her, barked again then bounded for the door.

"Not yet, Bozie." She answered him while pulling open the ammunition drawer. Hmm, take it all? Two boxes seemed a bit much just to get to town with so she left one in case someone might need it, another hapless hunter perhaps? Or she may decide to rent out her home while she was away. Jessa left the rifle and cartridges to go to her bedroom to dig out Grant's old duffle bag that his dad had given him, while saying "Keep it in the family." When his son had left home with his bride.

"Mr. Franklin was a real kick." Jessa had often thought. Although years ago, as she remembered, when she was a teenager dating Grant she thought her beau's father was maybe a bit, senile? Come to find out though it was the genetic strain of humor that the Franklin men shared, possibly scary? And she smiled at her memory of that first diagnosis.

And then there was Grant's mother. Mrs. Franklin was a virtual saint. While raising her own four children and working a full time job in county government she also taught Sabbath school for toddlers in their local church, and would invite visitors to her home for dinner afterward. The house was kept surprisingly clean in spite of all this, and in the summer there was a huge and well-tended garden also. After retirement, she volunteered in Community Services at her church, handing out clothing, bedding, household items, food, utensils, and occasionally money for those in need. Eventually and of course she took over the running of the operation, and whenever her church called upon her to head up a fundraiser, or to organize a disaster plan with the local fire station, she jumped right in with both feet first. Jessa had great respect for her mother in law, for Mrs. Franklin knew how to be in control of any situation given her, and it was because of this that Jessa was eternally grateful to the God of heaven that her wonderful husband had insisted that they move to another country to live.

But now she wondered how Bess was handling things. Did <u>she</u> know where Grant was?

Jessa brought the old duffle to the front room and tossed it onto the couch before opening it up. It was thick and tough, made of the strongest canvas material and big enough to hold herself if she had wanted to climb into it. She knew this for a fact because she had surprised Grant one fine birthday by hiding in it.

Next Jessa brought out her saddlebags, opened the right side and put in the rifle cartridges. Then she pulled open the drawer containing the dusty handgun and its extra bullets. Checking the safety of the pistol, she loaded it and the bullets, and then the flashlight and extra batteries would fill it. On the left side saddlebag, she packed a lunch with can opener and fork. She yanked the straps to pull them tight and buckled each one.

Into the duffle bag Jessa packed some dry papers, kindling for starting a campfire and a small metal box containing matches. It should not take much more than half the day to reach the lodge by horseback if she kept up the pace, for her animals were in top condition and were used to the trail ahead...still, if anything went wrong she would want a fire for company, as she would not be able to sleep, but only watch for things in the night.

She could have chosen the quad to haul her and her belongings but that would mean she would have to also carry the chainsaw, for these blustery days of late would surely have blown many a branch and even trees onto the path, which a bike simply could not hop over the way a horse can, and a living creature is better company than a machine no matter how useful. She did not like to think of operating the saw alone, either. One mistake and she could be bleeding, possibly to death and all alone. Jessa had learned one thing in this life in the wild, and that was to expect the unexpected and be prepared for it. On that note she found the trauma kit in the kitchen and shoved it into the duffle along with the flare gun, rain slicker, and her ratty leather gloves. Then it was time to think of other things so she stepped outside and trotted to the outhouse. While inside she said goodbye to the hanging basket of wild flowers, mostly blue Bachelor's Buttons. She thanked them for cheering her on these many lonely days. When she came out of the little building Jessa carried the basket to the river for a drink and some unexpected sunshine. The fresh air would perk them up.

Next she needed to feed the horses so that they could eat while she finished packing, so Jessa followed her bounding dog to the barn. The horses were not inside so she whistled for them and called them by name, to which momentarily their thundering hooves answered. Jessa and Bozeman raced to get out of the way as Samyra (Sameera) and Rory came galloping around the corner of the barn, heads tossing and rearing up at each other to show off for their audience. Jessa threw hay into the manger for them, and then added a quart of grain for each. As they munched away happily she slipped a halter onto each head and attached ropes, which were clipped to a large metal ring in either end of the manger. Jessa patted them and brushed their thickening winter coats until smooth, then picked their hooves clean of any debris. Good, all eight steel shoes were still tightly on.

Then Jessa and Bozeman left the steeds to their meals and headed to the chicken coup to gather their own breakfast by raiding the eggs. The chickens did not seem to mind as long as the dog stayed outside and they were fed for their trouble. Jessa came away with enough eggs that she and Boze could each have two of them scrambled with the last of the potatoes. This time when she left the coup Jessa fed her fowls extra grain, and closed their little house up tightly while saying "Go to sleep now girls. I will send someone for you if it comes to that." And walked to the house with the eggs in her shirt, feeling that her hens would be safe from coyotes for a while at least. They had food and water and would sleep most of the time since it was dark inside. Bozeman looked with his ears up at Jessa and at the eggs being held in the bottom of her shirt, so temptingly at the same level as his mouth.

After washing up and having breakfast Jessa took to cleaning the cabin. After all, what woman wants people to see her house left a muss? In case she never came back, that is. With that done she went to the safe and got money, credit card, phone card, address book, passport, and just in case, the map and compass. The duffle was getting full. She looked around her small home and a lump formed in her throat. 'No! No time for that now, must keep moving, and thinking clearly! She added wool socks to the bag and put on a leather belt in case a strap on a saddle broke or a rope, (besides, her jeans had become so loose) you never know. While rummaging around, her hand touched their family bible. It was the one her parents had given them on their wedding day. Lovingly she closed the cover, put it in its own case and squeezed it into the duffle. Then adding a small belly bag containing a toothbrush and paste, hairbrush, a hairclip, lip balm, folding scissors, and in case of a sliver, tweezers and hydrogen peroxide in a tiny squirt bottle. She carried a pocketknife in her jeans and Grant's hunting knife in its sheath fit nicely inside her boot.

She felt loaded for bear. Perhaps it was a mistake but she went back to her bedroom and opened the closet to take down her hat, and then saw the dresses hanging there. They seemed to stare back at her. She had not given any thought to dressing once she got back to where people were. How long had it been since she had worn one? Well, there were two birthdays every year, and they dressed up for Christmas in the cabin those two years they could not get to Montana because of the weather. And there were some lovely nights that simply waxed romantic. Bozeman spent those nights outside when Grant would come to the door in his tuxedo, carrying a beautiful bouquet of hand picked wild flowers and a disarming smile. Jessa would meet him at the door in her favorite mid length, midnight blue flowered cotton dress with the white lace, scooped neckline, also all smiles and wanton looks. After dinner Grant would serenade her with his guitar, not necessarily still in his tux.

Jessa smiled warmly at the memory as she gazed at his guitar case poking out from behind the bed. She leaned over and picked it up, then held it as if it were he in her arms. Suddenly trying to hold back her tears, Jessa snatched down the dress from its hanger, shook the dust from it and shoved it inside the case. Quickly she carried them to the couch and picked up the saddlebags to fling over her shoulder and the duffle bag to half carry, half drag to the front door.

Setting down her burdens for a moment she turned to look around her little home once more for anything else that may need to be brought out and noticed a patient friend waiting its turn for attention. A friend who knew her moods and needs, her small Spinet piano that had been painstakingly brought here and had done so much to keep her company. Jessa ran a caressing hand over its keys before closing the lid. "Thank you my friend." She heard herself say as she lowered the lid. Jessa then wrote a short note to leave on the Spinet, telling "Whomever it may concern, I have left my home in search of my life partner and do not know if I will come back. Use this home and its goods as it fits your need. Signed, Mrs. Grant Franklin." Picking up her load again a misty eyed Jessa headed to the barn.

Samyra, whose name Jessa had been told meant godmother, and her cohort Rory, whom Grant had bought for himself on his friend Ian's advice, were finishing their breakfasts. Rory was tipping his big head this way and that, trying to lick up the last hint of any grain. Jessa would load the pack frame on him first then the duffle bag and lastly the guitar case. She patted the big red dun's stout neck and shoulders and kept up a quiet conversation with the Quarter horse as she tightened the girth and belly straps of the cross-barred pack frame. Rory was a gentle powerhouse, willing to do most anything asked of him and did not get excited about much on the trail as long as he could follow Samyra. Now he was ready to do exactly that.

After placing the saddle on her petite mare's milky cream back and pulling the girth strap in to snugness, Jessa placed her horse's shapely Arabian head into her snaffle bit bridle and buckled the chinstrap. Lovingly Jessa scratched inside Samyra's ears for her, a place she could never quite get to herself (not even with Rory's help), and then she led the two horses out of the corral and took one last look around for anything she might need.

Bozeman loved it whenever Jessa caught cabin fever and had to go for a ride, so he was excited now at seeing the horses equipped to go. He liked them and they seemed to appreciate his guardianship, after all, they were part of what was 'his' and so he looked out for them as well. He and Rory often enjoyed a game of tag in the pasture, although the mare deemed it an unworthy sport when played with one of a non-equine persuasion, and even now Samyra treated Bozeman as if he had only recently tangled with the skunk.

Jessa led the horses to the river for a drink and while there she filled her canteen from upstream. The little company then came back up to the hitching post by the barn where Jessa tied them there and she slipped the strap of the canteen around the saddle horn and stepped away, to have one last look around. She had placed the pistol in the holster under the canteen, everything seemed ready, and yet something was missing. In that quiet moment she knew and kneeled to pray.

Though it had been some time since seeing this, Bozeman remembered what to do. He lay down with his head on his front paws, and closed his eyes.

Beginning with "Father in Heaven, Abba..." Jessa prayed for strength, wisdom, forgiveness and hope. She prayed that wherever her husband might be, and for whatever reason he was still there, that he would still love her as she still loved him. Then she prayed for protection in finding him, wherever he was. Lastly she prayed on behalf of others who knew and loved Grant to be strengthened also. Ending with "...in Jesus' precious name, Amen." Then the woman stood up and so did the dog, and she at least felt better. Stepping up into the saddle, Jessa turned her little mare to the bridge and to her future.

CHAPTER THREE

MEETING IAN

"Let's go, Sam." Jessa urged her horse across the bridge which connected the Franklin property (or, 'speck of land' as the neighbors referred to their seventy-five acres) with the Fuller's five generation ranch, farm and lodge, which was built by Josef and Evelyn Fuller some twenty five years ago. Each generation has its legacy and theirs was no different.

The mare was reluctant to attempt the bridge unless encouraged, for she simply could not get used to the deep hollow sound it made under her hooves, although she did her best to tip toe across it. But then came Rory on her heels with his heavy "Thump! Thumpa thumpa, thump!" Samyra may have thought him an insensitive clod, but to her credit she never said so.

Once across, it was up the first of three progressively higher hills, for Grant and Jessa's home was nestled in a tiny secluded valley all their own.

She did not dare to look back; she could only look ahead to the trail and wonder where it would lead her over these next few days and for the rest of her life.

The morning was still young for she had wakened with the sun and she felt good about her decision to go and find her husband. He was not the kind of man to leave her hanging like this, that is, not knowing. For her, their marriage was "...until death do us part." And she believed it was the same for Grant.

They had cleared the first hill now and dipped down a

bit, then back up for a steeper climb. Another half hour and they would be heading down toward the river again, they were making good time and the sun would be high when they reached it. Good, it would not be so misty and cold, and by then the horses would be ready for a rest.

Bozeman scared up a rabbit and her mare shied which stopped Jessa's planning. Boze, although being huge and usually bounding could also streak like lightning when motivated. Jessa saw them race to the brush, heard a "squeak" from the rabbit, then a few gulping sounds from Bozeman. She did not stop the horses for that. Knowing full well that the massive mascot could take care of his meals himself was encouragement and comfort to her. "If only it were so easy for me." Jessa said aloud, smiling down at her dog when he emerged from the underbrush to rejoin the little troupe.

Jessa meant to arrive at Fuller Lodge well before dusk, explain her situation and ask them to care for her horses and chickens until she could figure things out. Then she would drive to town and hop a small plane to the airport. She and Bozeman could be in Montana by tonight, a thought that usually made her heart sing, but not today.

The Fullers had more or less stumbled onto a profit-making sideline years ago, that of taking hunters on safari. This helped the ranch by keeping the bear and wolf population at bay for the sake of their cattle. Word of mouth eventually brought in enough hunters to require the assistance of more and more of the ranch's attention and personnel. She was sure they could use her horses for those wanting to do things the old fashioned way as she was doing now.

Jessa found herself wondering if Ian would want to care for her animals after what had happened yesterday. She forgave him but wondered if he would ever show her his face again. Though he had made the odd mistake she still trusted him, although if they ever found each other alone again, well that won't be happening now. She could forgive him for slipping up once, after all he had not seen or heard from Grant in even longer than she had. "He has surely decided his friend has either died or become a jerk!" She realized aloud.

The trail opened up now and left the trees behind it. "One more rise, Sam." Jessa said to the puffing horse beneath her. Sam's bobbing head leaned into the climb and meticulously she picked her way up the trail to the summit of the ridge. Her horse's snowy coat was steaming now from the exertion in the cold air and Jessa could hear the gelding puffing along behind them.

They had gone about four miles when from high overhead Jessa heard a falcon cry; a beautiful sound if you did not happen to be a rodent. At the bird of prey's scream, the great dog's ears jerked to attention. His eyes caught sight of the bird and followed it. Bozeman knew what a bird of prey was, and if he could outrun the falcon's killer power-dive and snatch up the whatever-it-was first he would have another meal. He also liked the competition. So he watched, muscles tensing, his one blue eye twinkling but the other more serious while the great bird folded her wings and dove.

Now! Racing at top speed Big Blue Bozeman was a blur, up over a fallen tree without losing stride he pounced as the falcon snatched up the snake, writhing and biting at the air while strong talons held it in check and powerful wings pushed them into the sky, its captor screeching all the while of the horror to come.

Poor Bozeman did not know what to think! He was perturbed that he had come up empty although he really was not looking to eat a snake, those nasty things were only good for tortuous throw 'em up games anyway. So he barked, a lot, and panted heavily. Then marked the spot and barked some more. Upset? Maybe, but by then it was time to catch up so as to lead the way, after all, those horses only knew best the way back to their own barn, as was his opinion. He could not understand their excitement about "heading back" for all he needed was food, water and Jessa. She was his 'barn' of comfort.

Jessa leaned back in the saddle as her horse squatted on its haunches for better traction and they maneuvered down the steep, winding slope to the clearing and the river, which she could now see for the first time since leaving her cabin home. Once there they could rest and eat. In another month the rains and snow would send the already rushing river over its banks and flood this little clearing, forcing travelers to use the less direct trail to the lodge.

"A glorious day!" Jessa gave her appreciation aloud and smiled as the warmth of the sun penetrated the cold spot under her wool-lined jean jacket. "It is always so beautiful here, no matter what time of year or whether the leaves are green, orange and red, or even dead and falling as they are now. If only Grant were here it would be perfect!" And she sighed heavily, for she knew that she had not truly faced the possibility of never seeing her husband again. But that time was coming for she felt it stalking her like an evil in the dark, waiting for her to make the odd mistake, and then...!

Samyra whinnied! Then Rory added his nicker of recognition. It was a greeting to a large yet elegant, coal black, proud cut gelding standing at attention with head and ears up, tail extended, muscles twitching and nostrils flared. As he screamed back another excited greeting and raced across the clearing toward them, Jessa reveled in his beauty and grace, as horses were her first love. Though the small valley echoed of his pride she was not afraid of him, this hurtling mass of muscle and hooves, for she knew him to be a gentle soul.

The great beast thundered up to Samyra and her rider with a rearing of front legs, and did no harm though Sam did squeal and paw the earth at him while raising her tail, even Rory snorted somewhat. After the ritual of snorting, stomping, and sniffing noses, the black horse turned on his heels to lope back to the spot of green he had been grazing on a few moments before.

This beautiful animal, 'Big J', had been foaled in an eastern province seven years ago to a popular racing mare. She was owned by a well known breeding farm that only had room for the rich and famous, who would be even more so by being perfect. Jessa swooned every time she saw him like this; free as any living thing can be, 'Big J' was the most beautiful animal Jessa had ever imagined.

But born with a hernia that made him appear to have something extra for the act of breeding, the owners decided he should be discarded, and the stable manager was given the order that by dark of night this innocent baby should be taken from his mother and hauled away by unmarked trailer and into the next province to be sold at a small town auction. The owner would announce that the foal had been stillborn and the mare bred back as soon as possible.

And so it was that two days later in a cold and muddy corral there lay a shivering, frightened and confused colt, who had done no wrong and yet was stripped of his mother's love and comfort. Frantic with hunger and aching for a friend he stood once again on wobbly legs to stretch out his neck and call for help, something he had done so often since being pulled and pushed into the trailer and taken from the only home he had known. Now his baby's voice which should have been growing stronger, was weakening as he noticed still yet another stranger looking at him.

Fortune smiled upon this needy creature when in the early morning hours of the auction that day Josef Fuller and his son were there in search of some farm equipment, and to sell an old Longhorn bull. They had been dabbling in Beefalo for a few years now because these animals proved hardier and more resilient to Grizzly bear attack than did the smaller Hereford cattle, and pound for pound were more edible than the older Longhorn breed.

It was Josef who saw him first, a pitiful, skinny, tiny dark lump with gangly legs and thin brush of a tail that when he stood up, stuck out defiantly. "Oh no." Josef said while leaning on the wooden fence rail to gaze at the colt. "That little feller can't be more than a few days old, and look at those ribs poking out! There ain't nothin' wrong with him I'll wager, just that little old bump under his belly that someone didn't like, he don't look 'fashionable' like that, y' know."

Ian had come over to look at the animal by this point, and seeing the orphaned waif he fell silent, on the outside.

Josef continued, "It's a shame. You know he'll go for glue and dog food on account of this time of year people aren't out for buyin' animals to feed through the winter unless they can pay for their keep. Just a cryin' shame, that's all." And Josef cocked his head to look at his son whose green eyes were fixed on the black eyes of the foal. The toddler bleated more than nickered, but it was enough.

"No he won't, dad." He said, and Ian strode to the office with a purpose in his walk.

A slow thin smile stretched across Josef Fuller's face as he recognized his son's intent. Ian generally said more with his actions than with words and Josef was proud of him. He would not mention that he would have done the same thing for the foal, for it was Ian who needed this scrawny, homeless and helpless creature, needed it desperately. Yes, his son had taken the bait, and Josef was relieved and proud of him.

And in a friendly way so was Jessa. She would be proud of anyone who would save an animal from needless destruction, she pondered as she looked around for 'Big J's rider.

Jessa had not disciplined her mount for reacting to him for she understood the basics of equine greetings and the need to establish an immediate 'pecking order' at every meeting. Only then could a herd live in harmony, the elder mare of the group would generally be the boss, until a younger and bolder one of experience and bad manners would push her way to the top, even if she were a petite little thing such as Samyra, the larger animals would submit to her herding instincts. When she deemed it time to get a drink in the pasture Sam would relate this to Rory by a nip from behind and 'herd' him to the creek. Also it was only okay to nibble her neck if <u>she</u> had an itch, then she would nibble his neck at just the spot where on her neck it itched. Then Rory would reciprocate. Teamwork, just as the stallion on the cliff is not there simply to look majestic, he is doing his part by watching for danger, or for other stallions coming too near 'his' mares. His mares only if he can keep them.

Jessa's eyes fell upon a log with an unusual lump on it.

Being curious she rode closer to the log and the river behind it. Then suddenly recognizing what it was she pulled in the reins more quickly than usual, causing Rory to walk into her mount abruptly.

It was Ian's saddle draped over the log, and so were his clothes. Gulp, Jessa swallowed and looked down. "Aah," She stammered. What to do? She did not <u>want</u> to look around, really. It would not be right to see him. So Jessa stared at her saddle horn and flushed when she heard splashing, shaking and running, then heavy breathing at her left stirrup.

It was Bonnie Blue Belle, a distant cousin to Jessa's own Blue Bozeman. Half the size and a few years older but every bit as energetic and willing, she too was a friendly soul to those she knew and trusted. Bonnie's eyes were both hazel and her long wavy hair ran mostly black to salt and pepper. Bonnie loved to help Ian and 'Big J' herd the livestock and was admired by other ranchers for her skill and endurance so much so that the Fullers had received many offers for her. Bonnie's owners would always smile graciously and simply say, "We just can't see selling a member of our family, thanks all the same."

Bonnie looked up at Jessa and lifted her right front paw to Jessa's boot. "Arf!" She barked, which clearly translated "Come down here and pet me!"

Jessa stayed in the saddle but reached down to pat Bonnie's head and scratch her ears, and the woman cupped the canine's face in her hand and asked the dog while looking her straight in the eyes, "Bonnie dear, where is Ian?" Immediately the herd dog dropped to the ground and spun around to race back to the river and disappear behind a boulder at its edge to announce "Arf!"

Jessa cleared her throat before calling out "Mr. Fuller, are you there?" After a moment she heard a rather sheepish reply from the rock, "Yes." it said. "And as you can see Mrs. Franklin, I am not quite in my altogether, so would you mind trotting off to the old oak tree down river and I will be along shortly?"

Jessa blushed as she gave a nudge to Sam and with a 'cluck' to Rory they trotted off down stream.

Ian had been out on the range since daybreak on the excuse that the southern fences had not been checked for breaks since the last windstorm. There could be stray livestock that had wandered onto the Franklin's 'speck'. But also he wanted some time alone to think about things and he liked the company of his horse and dog better for that than that of people, for humans tended to talk more than listen, and they always seemed to carry around their own agenda of personal problems.

And now <u>she</u> was here. By midmorning Ian realized he had been systematically working his way closer to the trail that led to her home. He had half hoped that the icy water would give him an inspiration, instead of the "Just passing by and wondered if you needed anything?" Pitiful, and now suddenly she was here and finding him like this.

Peeking over the top of the big rock that had so suddenly become his sanctuary, he asked of it "What could make a man become so stupid as to leave a woman like her?" To a man like Ian it seemed impossible. She was bright, loyal, brave and strong yet pleasant, and oh yes, beautiful! Grant, whom Ian used to think of as the smartest man he knew, next to his own father, must be the worst idiot on the continent to have left her like this! Ian shook his head as he raised his shivering, dripping body out of the frigid water and stepped onto the riverbank to dry and dress.

When he rode up on 'Big J' they were an impressive sight, each an excellent physical representative of his own species. Ian's long legs wore black jeans and black leather boots. His tan cowhide jacket was open at the top to reveal its wool lining and red and black flannel shirt over his red undershirt. His black cowboy's hat matched his wet wavy hair so well that it was difficult to tell where one left off and the other began.

Bonnie and Boze decided now would be a good time for a joint hunt and off into the brush they went, sniffing and snuffling at the thousands of scents to sort through.

Jessa had dismounted when she reached the far side of the old oak and took her horses to the river bank for a drink, then back to the smaller trees at the far side of the majestic giant to tie them there. She then removed Samyra's bridle, leaving the horse in the more comfortable halter. Next Jessa loosened the girth strap on the saddle and went to Rory to loosen his as well. Opening the left side of her saddlebag she took out her lunch and walked over to the log and stump by the oak. She set the can on the stump for a table and proceeded to take off her heavy jacket and hat, as now the day was comfortable enough to go along without them. At the sound of 'Big J's loping hooves she looked up at them and could not help but grin at Ian. "Hello, Mr. Fuller! Lovely day for a swim! And how was the water?"

Seeing her grinning up at him he had to smile back as his leather clad hands gripped the saddle horn and he swung down to land lightly on the ground. He tied the reins to the horn of the stock saddle to allow 'Big J' to wander, knowing the horse would not stray far from him.

Ian mocked a shiver for her, "Brrr! It's been warmer, I'll say that much!" He appreciated her ability to break the ice for him, something he always seemed to have trouble with. "Jessa, I am sorry for what I did yesterday, I overstepped and it was totally uncalled for, please forgive me?" She was touched at his sincerity and responded, "It's all right, neighbor, and I already have. And I can understand why you might think of me as possibly, available? In fact I hope I haven't done or said anything to make you wonder?"

He shook his head thoughtfully "Not at all."

Jessa exhaled at that. "Good. Because I am <u>not</u> and I will go on thinking that way until I know for a fact otherwise. Knowing that, I am sure you won't make the same mistake twice, right?" She asked with one eyebrow raised.

Ian was surprised at how relieved he felt. "Right!" He said, and then added "Thank you! I needed that!" And he walked away smiling as he patted 'Big J's rear-end and opened his own saddlebag to pull out a lunch sack and return to the log. Then he too took off his heavy coat and hat, though his still damp hair clung to the sides of his head. "I see you have Grant's guitar on the pack frame there." He said as he pulled out a sandwich bag.

"And your duffle is full instead of empty." Ian was about to take a bite of his sandwich, mouth open, then slowly lowered his hand as apprehensively he stated more than asked, "You are going in for more than supplies, aren't you?"

Jessa nodded, eyes downcast. "Yes, I have to. I have to know. Until then I cannot live." Then she looked up at him and directly into those searching green eyes to continue. "I feel as though I have stopped in time and cannot break through its barrier. I am a prisoner!" She didn't mean to, it was not planned, but a tear ran down her cheek as others followed and she turned away from him and sobbed. Jessa's shoulders shook until Ian's big gentle hands held them, then turned her around to be pulled into his strong arms. She responded by holding on to him and crying out her pain and suffering. He did not say a word for he was weeping too, hurt that she was hurt, hurting over the friend he had lost in Grant, and aching that Jessa would be leaving now when they might have become closer.

Awakened by the midday sun, the horses' legs stomped and tails swatted at buzzing 'Bull' flies landing on them to bite at their hides. The dogs had returned to the shade of the oak to pant and rest, then trotted to the river to lap up its refreshing water. A falcon cried from high above, causing the canines to once again race away through the trees.

The two mourners parted slowly, reluctantly, for neither had been held, really held, in a long time. They sat on the log face to face now, and for the first time as friends, for all else had been washed away. For a while nothing more was said and only their sniffles related anything at all. Then Ian broke the silence.

"I will go with you Jessa. I will make sure your place is taken care of until we get back, that is, when you want to come back and I pray God that you will. I can't let you do this alone."

A great relief filled Jessa's soul. "Thank you, thank you so much!" She managed through her sniffles and seeing his eyes were red from tears also, she smiled up at him while stating, "I packed food, weapons, clothing and bandages, but no tissues." And she laughed softly, causing a laugh and a grand smile from

Ian for which she rewarded him, "You know what, Ian? When you smile like that you are quite dashingly handsome, perhaps you could do it more often now?"

Jessa had never before seen a full-grown man blush. "What a refreshing sight," she marveled inwardly "like looking at a newborn baby, so very innocent and pure, something wonderful to behold!"

"Screee...!" Ian looked up to the clear blue sky above them, stood and raised an arm to the air, and what was once a wild thing came soaring to it and landed on it! With great talons grasping firm enough to cling yet not to tear, the bird of prey stared fiercely at Jessa (whose mouth fell open and eyes popped wide), at her horses, and most especially at Bozeman who had come bounding up to the oak tree ahead of Bonnie. Both dogs were panting hard from the effort of racing the great bird.

"Bonnie, lay down." Ian commanded, and as she did so Bozeman followed suit.

Jessa still had not found her voice, and was not sure she wanted to move a muscle quite yet, so Ian broke the ice for her this time.

"Ladies, allow me to introduce you. Jessa Franklin, please meet Fiona Fuller." He bowed low causing the bird to expand her wings for balance, which in turn caused Bozeman to growl at her, as she was posturing menacingly near his mistress. The bird screamed fiercely back at the dog and Jessa shushed him also. Boze decided he was outvoted when Bonnie "Arffed!" at him too. He lay with his head on his paws, but his ears were up.

Now Jessa found her voice. "How did you ever...?" And she motioned to the falcon that rested on his arm.

Ian explained. "It happened after the storm we had three weeks back when I was out clearing trails of the windfalls. Bonnie got to sniffing around all excitedly about something, then before I know it she is in a dog-fight with this screaming banshee of a falcon, and I can't tell who is getting the worst of it! Well of course I don't want my dog to get her eyes pecked out, so I step into it thinking I will simply hold the thing by its talons, and everything will calm down, yeah right!" And at that,

Ian slowly removed his gloves before continuing. "She did this to me even with a cracked wing."

Jessa inhaled sharply, "Oh, Ian!" For he still had deep, thick, dark red scratches on his hands from that first encounter with the falcon.

"Anyway, I tied her legs up good with some leather strips I always carry, and as gently as I could I slid her into my saddlebag with her head poking out, because she is too big to fit all of her in it. Otherwise I would have shoved her screaming beak in there too! If I'd had more strips I would have shut her up! 'Big J' certainly proved himself that day, because she screeched and screamed all the way back to the barn, and I thought my own ears would ring all night!" Ian gave a twisted grin at the memory as he shook his head. "Well, after I let mom treat these scratches, I put miss Fiona into a chicken cage in the barn and let her go hungry for the night, thinking she would be more polite the next day. Wrong again! She made it clear that when she found her freedom, the only dead meat she wanted was me!" And he grimaced. "Anyway, I slipped a tray of water in for her, and wriggled my knife through the cage wires just so, so that I could slit the straps off of her legs. She would not drink in front of me! But when I came back after chores the tray's water level was lower. After that it seemed she eyed me, although only slightly so, but less angrily. And the next day our orange barn cat Maxi, who is an excellent mouser and mother, brought me a half dead mouse and dropped it at my feet, purring all the while as if she knew that was what I had been wishing for, you know?" And Ian laughed, "Feline intuition? Anyway, I opened the cage door just enough so I could squeeze this poor dying rodent through and latch it before she caught my already sore hands. Even through gloves she can peck hard enough to hurt, she taught me that all right! But she would not eat it with me watching, even as famished as she must have been. Such a stubborn beauty, aren't you, 'Fi'?" Ian asked of the bird perched on his arm, her wings folded now and her piercing black eyes stared directly at him as if to say, "Well, go on!" And so he did.

"I could tell she felt frantic with hunger as well as the rest of her situation, so I left her until the next day, and I believe you can guess that there was no evidence of a mouse ever being in that cage. No bone or hair, no whiskers or tail, 'nada'. She is a neat freak, my Fiona." And Ian caressed the bird's beak and head with a finger, then noticed Jessa's quizzical look. "Oh, the name? You may not know this about me, Mrs. Franklin, but I happen to be a fan of the older generation movies. Perhaps it is from living with my parents and grandmother, but also there is a certain respect for life and dignity in them that is rare and sadly lacking in movies of our own generation, or books for that matter.

One of my favorites is about a wealthy businessman from the big city who travels to Ireland with a friend to do some hunting, and they hike along until they come to this misty valley. The people in it are waking from a one hundred year sleep brought upon them by a blessing from God, that they may live forever without being corrupted by outside influences. Living in the village is a beautiful woman named Fiona, and she and the hero fall in love. But all too soon the village begins to fall asleep again and he flies back to his life in the city, only to find that he cannot get her out of his mind." And at that Ian glanced at Jessa who sat mesmerized by his oration. He continued. "And so he returns to the sleeping village to be near her for as long as possible, and finds the power of their love is strong enough to allow him to join the sleepy band of time travelers. The hero chose to forsake the life he knew to be with the woman he loved for one waking day of every century. I believe love is worth that." And Ian gave Fiona a lift into the air. Powerful wings, though one was still wrapped for support, brought her swiftly back to lofty heights. He watched her go, and as he had so many times, hoped it would not be the last.

Jessa, whose eyebrows had been raised for a very long while, watched her go as well, then incredulously demanded "Ian Fuller! <u>Why</u> aren't women lined up at your door? It's a puzzle to me now more than ever!"

He hesitated, "Well, they're only allowed on holidays." And he tried to smirk, but sobered instead. A pained look attacked his chiseled face as he confessed. "There was one once, and right away I was quite taken with her. My friends were taken with her too. Things were getting so serious that I brought her home for Christmas and introduced her to my family. Then that New Year's morning, after a late night party in the banquet hall downstairs, my brother," and Ian whispered the name "Kent, took me aside on my way to the kitchen and said 'Ian get your coat. I've got something to tell you, outside.' And Jessa, I swear to you the hair on the back of my neck stood straight up!"

Jessa did not say a word for she was afraid to, for the back of her own neck was having a similar reaction.

Ian continued. "We walked outside onto the snowy yard, and it has been eight years, but I still remember the cold sting in the air. It was nothing compared to the sting of my brother's words."

"'Ian', he'd said, 'you are my brother and I love you, please remember that! But somehow I have fallen in love with Kathryn and last night I went to her room, and slept with her. I will be the one marrying her, not you. I'm sorry for you, and I hope that some day you can find it in your heart to forgive us.'"

"Oh my God." Jessa whispered. "How could anyone do that? And to someone they loved?"

After gathering himself Ian continued. "I had never known rage in my life before this. It is a red-hot monster that took control of me, body and soul. I was bigger than my brother even then, and with one hand I grabbed into his flesh so hard he couldn't escape while the other formed a pulverizing fist! 'Bam!' I hit him hard and pulled back for more because right then at that moment, it felt *good* to release my anger on him and I had so much of it, it *had* to be released! 'You pig!' I screamed at him. 'How could you do it? How could you do this to me? You've ruined everything! My *life*! And my fist found his bloody face again. This time he fell unconscious to the ground. Well, a minute later the lights came on all over the lodge and cabins, people came out to see what all the commotion was about and could not believe their eyes. They were curious but nobody seemed to want to get too close. They didn't need to worry though, I was numb all over, stunned as if I had been the one on the ground. Pretty soon I realized mom was crying over Kent and calling for a first aid kit. I stood over him then to take a look at what I'd done, panting at first, then I took to bawling like a baby and hoping my brother would be alright, although I was sure I had broken his nose.

Kathryn had been in the shower when the chaos started. Her long brown hair was dripping in ringlets on her rose colored bathrobe when she peered through the crowd on the porch, and looked me right in the eyes, searching me inside. I think she was afraid that she might be next." Ian winced at the thought while shaking his head and stating, "But I had never struck a woman and was not about to start with the one I loved. Well I guess she figured me out because she ran right over to hold Kent's bloody head on that pretty robe of hers, and that pretty much explained it to everyone there. To my dad and to my mom, but I still didn't get it. How could the woman I love, who said she loved me, and my own 'Let's go fishin', yeah, you can borrow my jeep and my new shirt too', brother, whom I loved as my best friend, why didn't they just say 'No!' when the time came? How would they be able to trust each other in their own relationship, knowing how they had come together?"

Jessa could only shake her head for she did not know either.

"Well, to get on with it," Ian continued "I _had_ broken Kent's nose but that didn't stop him from moving away with Kathryn to the far northeast corner of the rangeland. They even started building a house there, of sorts. You want to know something, though? Kent was the smart one of the Fuller brothers and he knew that if he fought back I might have killed him, so he took those punches and let that rage flow out of me. Well, it didn't take long before I missed him, and even forgave him, but not soon enough." And Ian whispered the last. "Because two months later a Mounty drove up to announce that," and now Ian's words came slow and hard "that Kent had been mauled by a bear, and died. I never took the chance to tell him I forgave him and still loved him, and wanted him to come home. We never saw or heard from Kathryn again, I didn't try to contact her." The tears streamed freely down Ian's care worn face now that he had spoken of his losses, and through choking words he finished his story.

"She didn't come to his funeral. It was a closed casket ceremony for he had been mutilated. The folks don't talk about him, at least not around me, but sometimes at night I hear ma crying, and dad trying to comfort her, and I know it's for Kent." And Ian could say no more.

Gently Jessa pulled him to her and held his head to her shoulder for a long time, wanting desperately to comfort her newly found friend in any way she could. He was too big to cradle in her arms or to rock him, so she simply held him there and wept with him for his horrific loss, for the family he would never have, and for his family that was left to go on without their beloved brother, uncle, son and grandson, he would have contributed much.

A chilling breeze swept through the clearing and shook loose a few remaining dead leaves from the oak tree's mighty branches, causing the only two people for miles around to shiver and realize that the season's weak and few remaining sun rays were fast fading. They released one another once again and donned their coats and hats. Their dogs came over to them and demanded attention, demanded they be allowed to comfort their masters. They were allowed. The dogs distracted the two humans long enough for them to listen to the noise they had been hearing but had ignored, their stomachs. They had started eating their lunches some time ago but had not gotten around to actually finishing. Now suddenly finding it late in the afternoon they agreed to finish quickly and head out. The days grew rapidly shorter this time of year and the nights could be bitterly cold.

After remounting their horses they trotted along the river's flat terrain for nearly two miles before slowing for the climb to a small plateau that would reveal the valley of the Fuller's lodge. They rested their animals there and dismounted to stretch their own legs and work out some stiffness in the knees.

Ian surveyed the remainder of their journey with binoculars. "Can't see too much of the valley, the fog is coming up. At best you and I will get in late tonight, you know? If we get that far! Penalty for sharing and caring, I guess." But he was smiling as he said it, Jessa could tell even though he was facing the ledge and not her, by the sound of his voice, for her friend was happy and relaxed around her now. Thinking about that she smiled to herself and felt good, for now she could understand better why the Fullers had seemed so distant before.

Through the binoculars Ian could discern a suspicious whiteness in the cloud emerging from behind a distant mountainside, "I'm glad you aren't traveling alone, kiddo." He said as he lowered the 'spy' glasses and handed them to Jessa while pointing to the far-off mountain. He explained why in one word, 'snow'".

Jessa breathed in, "Oh, how beautiful!" Then more urgently she quipped, "Let's get moving!"

They practically jumped onto their horses and turned to trot to the far end of the plateau, where there was a steep descent to a lower ridge, which would eventually drop them to the valley floor, a short distance from the lodge. Fortunately for them the cloud they had seen hovered at the mountain's side and dropped its load there, before breezing on past their plateau that evening. Winter was to pounce on them soon enough, and it would not come alone.

Near the base of the plateau Ian turned 'round in the saddle to check up on Jessa and her little company as he often did, however discreetly so she might not feel insulted, and noticed that Rory was limping on his back right hoof. "Uh oh! Your packer has a sore there, let's get down to this camp sight and check him out." And as he said so Jessa could make out a circle of rocks and flattened grass where hunters had used the area.

Looking back at Rory, Jessa could also tell he walked with a bit of a limp now. Hopefully it was just a rock in the frog, which could easily be pulled out with a hoof pick.

They rode to the camp and dismounted, and then tied

their horses to the trees that surrounded the fire pit. Jessa was glad for the protection from the wind, as the open plateau had offered no such shelter. She went around Rory's rear-end now and tugged on his fetlock hairs, saying "Up, Rory." And the gentle animal lifted his tender hoof for her inspection. Sure enough he had picked up a large, sharp stone that was now embedded between frog and shoe. Luckily with a little prying of the pick and a grunt of effort from Jessa the rock dislodged and went flying to 'clack!' against the ring of bigger rocks that had held many fires. She patted Rory's butt and put her pick back in her pocket.

"Is he okay?" Ian asked as he stood up from petting the dogs.

"Well, the stone was sharp enough to lodge in tightly and cause a tender spot, but I think he will be alright. Still, maybe he should not have to trot so much. We have been making pretty good time to make up what we lost, could we walk the rest of the way and still be alright?" Jessa asked hopefully.

Ian gave it some thought. "No, I'm sorry. We either have to keep pushing to make it tonight, or we should make camp right now because this is the best spot for shelter between here and home. And if we decide to go on, remember this, the sun will be going down at precisely the time the trail ends to become that rutty old logging road that washes out this time of year, and it would be foolhardy to attempt it in the dark. I vote to stay put."

Jessa knew it was the smart thing to do, as she stood there looking at him. And yet, there were social issues.

"You trust me, don't you?" He asked as if hurt.

"Yes! She quickly responded. It's not that, I do trust you Ian. But not in my wildest dreams would I have predicted that things would have come to this. I was so certain that I would be at the lodge, or in town, maybe even at my folks', tonight I mean.

Ian's eyes drifted to the duffle bag on Rory's back. "Jessa, did you pack a bedroll?"

She bit her bottom lip in answer.

"Oh." He exhaled slowly. "Well, we can't go any farther tonight. I have my bag and a tarp. We will sleep on the tarp and have the bag open on top, and sleeping in our clothes of course." He cleared his throat. "Body heat should suffice since we are in a spot the wind can't reach so well, and at least there is a soft grassy spot, we won't be on rocks, I've done that and it is no fun! Chin up, we will be okay and I will keep a fire going through the night. We just won't bring it up in conversation about the sleeping arrangements when we get back now, will we?"

Jessa shook her head quickly and smiled in relief. "I like to think of myself as a person who thinks ahead in order to be prepared, but I sure blew it this time, didn't I?"

"Hey, don't beat yourself up over the small stuff, there is no way you could have expected to meet some dopey naked guy in the river! I was surprised you didn't simply gallop on out of there instead of waiting to talk. Thank you for being brave enough to trust me." And Ian rewarded her with one of those dashing smiles.

"You are welcome." Jessa replied royally, then turned away from him on pretense of bedding down the horses, for she did not want him to see her crimson cheeks.

Jessa stripped her horses of their burdens as Ian cared for 'Big J'. Normally he would allow the animal to roam free during their campout but tonight there would be other horses to mess with and ropes to entangle, and after all 'boys will be boys' no matter what the species. Next Ian took 'Big J' to the river for a drink and as he brought his horse back up the embankment, Jessa was bringing her two down to quench their thirsts from the work of the afternoon.

All of the animals were tired and the horses each took to rolling after they were unloaded, in order to work out the sweat and itches caused by the saddles and pack frame. Even the dogs were content to stay put for a time, for even though the day was cool their long, thick and furry hair had kept them quite warm with all of the day's activity. Jessa brought her horses up from the river to tie them to the trees at a distance apart from each other so that they could not cross their ropes.

A moment later she heard an axe chopping through wood and turned around to see Ian at work preparing chunks for the night's fire. That gave her the idea to pick up limbs for kindling and get the fire started, so she wandered through the trees for what had fallen from the branches above, and went back to the fire pit with her bundle. They would need more than this small pile, so she headed back to venture farther as things had been pretty well picked clean by the hunters who had camped there previously. Jessa listened contentedly to the sound of the chopping as she hunted her sticks until it stopped for a few moments, and then resumed. Upon returning to the pit she could see why, for Ian had removed his shirts.

Jessa knew it made sense not to work up a sweat before bedding down in the chill night air, "Perfectly sensible" she whispered to herself. She stood there with her load of sticks, watching as powerful muscles rippled with his every swing of the axe. Each swing sent bits of wood flying through the air. It was fascinating to watch him. "If only it were Grant..." the words escaped her lips before Jessa realized it and suddenly she shook herself and dropped her load into the fire pit, then searched her duffle for the tin of matches and dried papers. Few moments passed before a wispy plume of smoke emerged from the sticks, then a small flame shot forth to claim the pit as its own.

Ian knew he might work up a sweat. Actually he wanted, no, needed to work hard. It was his way of gathering his thoughts and studying them while his physical focus was on a task at hand, that of getting through this night as a gentleman.

He approached the pit now with shirts intact, and dropped his first armload of split wood, spun on his heels and went back for more, leaving Jessa to feed the fire. When he returned for the fifth time there was an eager fire and an impressive stack of wood.

"That should do us for one night." He announced, and checking the position of the sun that hovered precariously above the western hillside he continued while gesturing to a thicket, "I will be using the west wing privy before turning in, if madam prefers the east wing?"

To which Jessa gave him a quirky smile as she responded, "Why yes, madam does." And she rose and stepped carefully down into a washout that provided a modicum of privacy without pushing through any thorny briers.

That duty being done, Jessa returned to the river to wash her hands and face. Looking around she spotted Ian rubbing 'Big J' and talking to him. The horse obviously loved him and did not like being tied away from him.

Ian joined Jessa at the river, and together they walked to the fire pit in the half-light of the evening. They talked at the fireside for a time, then it was time to turn in, and by the light of the early stars, a half moon and a fire, they made their bed.

First Ian laid down the tarp on what was the thickest patch of grass. Next he tossed down his sleeping bag, unrolled and unzipped it then spread it out on top of the tarp. He sat down on the left side to remove his boots, and then slipped inside. Resting his head on his saddlebag pillow Ian said without looking at her "Goodnight, Jessa." And he pulled his hat down over his eyes.

Jessa stood looking at her side of the bed. She looked at the fire, at the horses, the dogs resting nearby, the trees, the moon and stars, and then at her boots. She sat down and took them off as he had done, and into the pod crept the second pea.

Then the first pea, which had its back to the second pea, spoke. "Comfy?" It inquired.

"I'm okay."

"Good." He piped.

"Goodnight." She said and pretended to fall asleep. Soon enough she was not pretending anymore.

Quietly Ian checked the position of his pistol inside his saddlebag pillow. 'Yes, right where I can get at it in a hurry.' He had noticed how Jessa had left her weapons too far away if there were an emergency, something he felt certain she would never have done if traveling alone. He had not mentioned it to her because it pleased him how she relied on him, if only subconsciously, to protect her. And she was right. He would do everything he could to do exactly that. "No matter what." He thought. "Even if it means handing her over to Grant?" Came a nagging thought. "You know his death has not been confirmed, he could resurface and beg her to take him back. Then what?" The thought continued. Ian looked at Jessa lying next to him and by the fire's glow he could see her face, finally relaxed from her many cares.

"No matter what." He said to the night, then fed the fire another chunk and went to sleep next to his friend.

CHAPTER FOUR

LANDSLIDE!

Thousands of miles away in the farthest reaches of the world, a rain-soaked scientist rechecked his probe's readout after looking in disbelief once again at the information sent him by satellite, while waiting impatiently below were the rest of his team members who now resorted to honking the jeep's dull horn and revving the engine. "Grant! It's got to be now or never! This whole mountainside is going to let go!" Cho called up to him with the loudspeaker. He stood, 'mic.' in hand, next to the jeep full of team members who were all waving and calling frantically up at Grant.

They were right of course, and he gathered his findings to slip and slide down the water saturated hillside in his once bright yellow rain slicker, hat and goggles now muddied to brown nearly blending him into invisibility.

The interpreter on the team who had hailed him was stepping back into the vehicle when it happened.

First came the rumbling. Rocks rolled past and trees uprooted, and then came the inevitable ride on moving earth. "Dear Jesus..." Grant began to pray as he caught one blurred glimpse of the jeep being covered in rocks, trees and mud, then heard a "thud" behind him, or in him perhaps. He could not know for all consciousness had ended.

CHAPTER FIVE

FULLER LODGE

Sometime later, around midnight he guessed, Ian awoke to a swirling breeze and startled a deer that had come to the river for a drink. He saw that the fire was nearly out, and rose to add kindling to revive it, then chunks of wood to bring it back to a crackling blaze. Through a sleepy haze in his brain he remembered why this modicum of heat was more important than at other times, and looked to his spread out sleeping bag where a slender form lay, her sleeping face now aglow from the light of the flames. He had known her from a respectful distance for several years, and now from a respectful closeness. He looked away from that endearing face to ponder and found himself hoping he would not one day regret becoming closer, as he had once only hoped for. He was certain he would not survive another emotional catastrophe, and thinking of his past experience, it was with a quiet fearfulness that he slid carefully back into their makeshift bed and back into sleep.

Hours later the black night turned to shades of gray, snuffing out the stars one by one as a pale orange hue heralded the coming of the lazy winter sun. It was chilling cold and Ian realized the fire was merely smoldering again. He moved quickly to rise up and wished he had taken his time. "Ow! I must be getting old!" The thought cried out as every muscle complained about the sleeping accommodations of the night.

Stoking the fire and building it to near bonfire proportions, Ian turned to where Jessa lay under the frosty bed. Aside from a narrow ridge that must be her body, the only indication she was there was an escaped fluff of her long dark hair waving at him in the breeze, for she had scrunched down undercover to escape the cold morning dew. Ian smiled at the fluff as he first pulled on his boots then headed over to the circle of trees where the horses were tied. He knew that no wild animals had bothered them because the dogs had not sounded any alarms during the long uncomfortable night. But sometimes a horse will get itself into trouble with the rope, or a tree branch, perhaps a hole. Fact is a horse will get itself into trouble if it has a mind to.

He came up to Rory first. The big sleepy gelding nickered low to him and put his muzzle into Ian's hands, searching for grain. Ian had liked Rory from the start, in fact he had been with Grant the day his friend had bought the big red dun on his own advice, that here was a gentle, willing powerhouse ready to be a friend to any kind person and especially useful to the novice rider that Grant was. And he had been right. It was a good match for Grant and now it proved to be a good thing for his wife who had to pack out like this. Ian patted the big animal as he untied him to lead to another grassy spot that had not as yet been devoured by the gelding. Immediately the horse was ripping up green and chewing. "Might as well go back to sleep 'Big Guy.'" Ian said as he yawned and moved on, then nearly fell over Bonnie who had come up quietly in the half-light of the morning. She was stretching and yawning, too.

Ian squatted low to pet his sleepy dog, which put a paw on his knee and licked his hands in mutual adoration. He heard the brush and branches shaking in Samyra's direction, and sure enough the mare had her rope wrapped under her front leg and could not set it down.

He came up to her slowly so as not to spook her, and speaking softly he said, "Well pretty lady, you timed that well enough." Sam allowed him to lift her leg to release the taught rope, then she put her head down into his hands, searching for grain to which Ian told her "Yeah, yeah, I know what you're after and as soon as we get you to the lodge you can have all the grain you want, 'Sam'". And Ian moved Samyra to a fresh spot of grass as well, and then he patted her milky hide and walked off to greet 'Big J'.

Generally when out on the trail Ian would leave 'Big J' untied, figuring that the swift and powerful horse could better defend himself from any of the large wildcats or bear in the area if he were free. But this night there had been other horses to mess around with and he did not want any broken halter, ropes, or bones for that matter.

His horse nickered to him as Ian came near. "Hi ya handsome." Was Ian's answer as he came up to his mount. "Did you sleep well?" And when his horse pawed the earth to be free, Ian responded "Well, neither did I, but I wouldn't have it any other way." Suddenly it dawned on Ian that soon he would have to leave for who knew how long, and would have to part from this loyal friend he had grown to love so much. "If only I could take you with me, J." And he hugged the sleek black neck and scratched the slope of the horse's powerful shoulders. Now Ian had something else against Grant.

After bringing 'Big J' down to the river for a drink, Ian retied him for a bit of horsetail breakfast. The plants had a lot to offer in bulk, and his horse liked them. He made a pit stop, and then washed before heading back to the fire and Jessa.

Arriving back at the bed which was now quite damp on top from the melting frost, the sun was fully up and yet he could see no movement from under the cover. Ian decided to let her sleep and told Bozeman, who had lain down next to his mistress sometime earlier in the grayness, to "Stay." Then with his own dog Ian went traipsing over the terrain to a hidden grove.

Bozeman lay his head back down on his paws once again though he did not close his eyes. His ears would twitch this way and that at the sounds of the man's footfalls, the brush being pushed about, the horses munching and stomping occasionally or a fish jumping in the river. Once he heard the screeching of a bird of prey but he did not race off after it this time. Eventually his mistress stirred from under the bag he guarded and he knew she would join him in wakefulness soon enough. Then he would race the bird again!

Under cover of the sleeping bag was hidden Jessa's rapid eye movement. She was dreaming of her husband once more. "Grant! Hold on!" She heard herself screaming, her hand reaching out for his as he fell from the precipice, his screams blending with her own. "Too late! Oh God, I'm too late!" A tear rolled down her face as she hung there, hand and arm reaching as far as they might, the echoes of his cry ringing in her ears. Then Bozeman was by her side, licking her face at the cliff's edge.

Jessa awoke to find her hairy friend once more coming to her rescue, saving her from her own torment by licking her salty, tear stained face as she knew that <u>it</u> had happened again. Looking around herself as consciousness returned, the old cliché of "Where am I?" escaped her lips. Then memory trudged along to fill in the gaps. She really was on her way to find him; that much was not a dream. Jessa sat up too quickly and realized her mistake instantly. Her back, head and neck, shoulders, butt and hips, knees, <u>everything</u> hurt! "Ow!" Came the exclamation and "I must be getting too old for this!" She grimaced and stood slowly as she listened to her angry empty stomach that had not even had its nightly tea before turning in. She pulled on her boots before stumbling to the fire, and then stood shivering with arms and hands outstretched to absorb its warmth. Her tummy roared again, causing her to take stock of her situation. "Well, Jess old girl," She stuttered through chattering teeth, "you are freezing, starving, aching, borderline psychotic," she wrinkled her nose before adding to the list "and you stink!" And yet, there was a certain personal satisfaction in taking action.

Looking to the horses, Jessa could see they all had been moved for a fresh meal in preparation for the last leg of the journey. Watching them eat did not help her own stomach any so she looked away. Having an idea to fill her need, she guzzled from the canteen in an attempt to fool her own demanding innards, which did work for a while; about two minutes worth.

Bozeman 'woofed' softly and with tail wagging trotted to a tunnel of sorts in the trees where Ian emerged with a cheerful

"Good morning, Sleeping Beauty! I've been out to a pear tree I know of, only because I planted it years ago so that there would be fresh fruit for myself and whoever…" Suddenly Ian realized she had been crying and lost his cheerfulness. "Did something happen?" And his eyes darted about the area in search of a culprit.

Hesitantly Jessa replied. "Not really, just my morning ritual of late is all." And to his questioning face she explained. "These past couple of weeks I have not had a night without waking up sometimes screaming, other times crying, or both. And it is always about Grant. At first it was a more than mild case of missing him because he has been gone longer than ever, longer than most wives would stand for I am sure."

Ian heartily agreed with her.

She continued. "But these last five nights have been different, more intense, and in each dream Grant is somehow being threatened by some frightening doom. I try so hard to save him but I am always too late! If I could only get to him sooner I could save him!" Her voice resounded in frustration.

He recognized her aching in body and soul for he had been there himself.

They stood in silence for a moment, then Ian handed his hungry-eyed companion (who snatched it up greedily) a pear, stating "We will be at my place in an hour and you can make some calls. I will explain it to my folks and instruct one of the hands to take care of your place temporarily, and if Jeff is still there we will have a flight out to the airport as soon as possible. When you find out a few things then you will know where to go and what to do, and knowing that will help some.

"Yes!" She slurped. "I've been thinking that too." And with that they ate the last of the fall pears and proceeded to break camp. Ian put out the fire with water and dirt, while Jessa loaded Rory's pack frame and moved on to saddling Samyra, as Ian saddled and then mounted 'Big J' to wait for his friend.

Stepping up into the saddle this morning Jessa's legs and bottom were sore and full of complaints, but she said nothing about it, as it seemed Ian was expecting some sort of remark. Jessa wanted him to think she was tougher than that.

And he was expecting, no, <u>hoping</u> for a mention of complaint, for he wanted to know it was not only he who felt the pains of the day. "Well, she is a little younger than I am." Ian thought when Jessa nudged her horse to start walking down the trail and without complaint. "I guess it's just me. It must be that last birthday I had. My friends warned me about turning thirty, I guess I have to believe them now."

The dogs took the lead toward the lodge now, which for Bonnie meant home. Bozeman did not care where they went for he was having a high time bounding here and there with Bonnie as they went snorting and sorting through the scents of the trail.

Jessa and her horses followed them at a brisk walk with Ian close behind to keep an eye on Rory, to be sure he did not develop a limp. After a time Ian felt convinced that the big gelding was sound, and when the trail opened to a wide spot he and 'Big J' soared on past Jessa with an exhilarating "Follow me!" As he sidetracked off the main trail for a less used path that zigzagged up the side of the last ridge before coming into the valley of Fuller Lodge.

From the height of the ridge Jessa could look over and see the vast spread of buildings that were Fuller Lodge. She smiled wistfully, saying, "There she is, and there my life will change."

Until this moment Ian had not realized the full impact that reaching his home would have on his companion. Now he could see it in her face, and he wondered what the next few hours would bring.

He began it by twisting around in his saddle to reach into the left side bag and extract the two-way radio he kept there. As he pulled out the long antenna, Ian smiled at Jessa, stating, "Don't leave home without it." Then pressing the 'mic.' button "Ian to Fuller Lodge, you copy?"

A pause, then a reply "Good to hear your voice, brother 'Eenny'! We expected you last night, come back."

Ian responded with a smile at Jessa and "I'm alright,

Lorene! It's good to hear your voice, sis. Welcome back! Say, I'm bringing in a friend of yours with me."

"Is it my Jessi?" Excitement filled the young woman's voice now.

"Yeah sis, you guessed it! And she is looking a bit peaked," (at that Ian glanced apologetically at Jessa, whose eyebrows had risen) "I want you and Ma to put out all the fixings today to perk her up, come back?"

"We copy that, fence rider! Bring her on in! Lodge out."

"Fence Rider out." Ian replaced the two-way in the saddlebag. Seeing Jessa's hopeful countenance, Ian explained, "She didn't know anything about Grant or she would have said so, and I'm guessing you know my sister about as well as I do."

Jessa felt disappointed, relieved and excited all at once. Her disappointment was obvious for she still knew nothing more about her husband's status. She was relieved at not hearing any bad news about him, and her excitement stemmed from hearing her girlfriend's voice and anticipation at seeing her again for the first time in over a year, since Lorene had married and moved to Alaska.

Lorene and Jessa had bonded practically on first sight of each other five years ago. These two young women who were so different physically, Lorene a towering, blonde haired brown eyed beauty (taking after her mother) Jessa a petite blue eyed brunette, yet each shared a common need, the company of another young woman, for there were few available on a regular basis in their area. The two giggled like sisters and could share things from common pet peeves to buried secrets of the heart. Jessa had sorely missed Lorene's company when her friend had married and moved, and now Lorene was visiting with her baby while her husband was away on another fishing excursion, that being their bread and butter. It was now Lorene's turn to feel the pangs of loneliness while her beloved was away.

Ian broke into her reverie with "Take us down Jessa, luxury awaits you now!"

"Sounds good to me!" Jessa exclaimed enthusiastically and

turned her horses around to head back along the switchback trail to meet with the flat ground once more.

Samyra seemed to think it was an awful nuisance to walk the same trail twice as she tiptoed in her half squat position for traction. Rory did not care, for nothing seemed to bother him as long as he could eat once in a while and follow his mare.

Big J. would have sailed on by them and on to his stall and the grain he would get there if his rider had allowed it, but Ian was content with watching to see how Jessa handled things. Her little mare fairly floated over the trail with each step carefully placed. He knew Jessa was in good hands, so to speak, by the way the horse held her head tilted down so as to study the ground, and her ears perched forward at attention. She had the intelligence about her that was needed in a good trail horse.

Studying her now reminded Ian of the first time he'd had the chance to watch her in action. It was this last summer when Grant had invited himself and Jessa to go along with Ian to ride fence, not the whole way, only three days' worth, but the three of them had become better acquainted. Grant had encouraged Ian to talk more freely, even in front of his wife, which was something he had felt uncomfortable with and now wondered why. Ever since then and especially recently, Ian could not help but wonder if it was because Grant had wanted him to take care of Jessa while he was away, to look after her if something should happen to him. 'Big J' stumbled over some loose terrain, thus jerking his rider's thoughts back to the present.

They reached the bottom of the ridge now and walked more quickly along the flat terrain where the trail widened, before breaking open upon an old logging road, which proved to be more rutty and slippery than the trail, and was the reason for not attempting to finish their journey during the night. The makeshift road followed the river for a short time, then broke away and headed straight toward the cluster of the lodge's outbuildings. The river veered left to flow near to the westernmost point of the largest of the buildings, which was the lodge itself.

Though the riders were able to sit abreast now because

the road was wider than the trail had been and so conversation would be physically easier now, they fell silent. There was only the sound of horses' hooves making sucking sounds as they lifted from the muddy road. The closer they came to the compound the heavier the silence became.

At a short distance from the nearest outbuilding, which was an equipment shed, there was a cattle grate. Constructed of steel bars and grating and painted bright yellow, any vehicle it would support and yet the odd stray bovine would look to it as it would a wolf or sinkhole, and avoid it instinctively. Horses would need urging to cross it until they became used to such an unnatural thing, that being walking over a hole rather than around it.

From a sideways glance Ian eyed Jessa and her horse. Would Sam balk at the crossing? It has been some time since she has had to use it, and Jessa looked so intently at it, was she about to urge her horse?

Unaware of her own intensity Jessa was thinking. "Fear is like that barrier. Fear of the unknown keeps us from stretching our talents and abilities. It has kept me cowering in the wilderness afraid to venture out and gather information because it might hurt to move on; afraid to move ahead, afraid of change.

Sam slowed and put her head down to the bright metal in her path to snort at it, then proceeded gingerly across the clanging thing with added spring in her already light step. 'Big J' showed no change in his long stride and Rory, well he didn't either.

Before reaching the equipment shed on the right, there was a sentimental marker to the left.

Glinting in the climbing morning sun that peeked through patches of cloud and mist was Ian's late great grandfather's prized model A Ford, the only car ever owned by a Fuller. To protect it a small open faced shed covered it above and on the western side. The eastern sunrise now bounced its rays off the refurbished black shine of metal and glass.

Further on and to the right was the equipment and tool

shed. Even larger a structure than the lodge itself it held a fleet of pickups, old and new. There were mountain bikes and quad motorcycles, haying equipment and tractors. On display was a huge harness and plow that had been used by Ian's also deceased grandfather to plow and pull stumps with in order to clear land for the compound. He and his wife Dora, who survives him, built the original lodge, which Ian's parents had added on to.

Passing the equipment shed they rounded the curve in the now rock driveway where it branched right to the stables and the way to town. They veered left and passed the steaming windows of the natural hot spring sauna and pool house.

Across from the pool house and behind a split rail fence was the helicopter pad and adjoining airstrip, which ended in a pond stocked with fish. Beyond the pond was an open meadow with large wooden picnic tables and space for campers. Twice a year the lodge played host to endurance riders, there were also Mounty gatherings and horse clubs, shooting clubs, motorcycle clubs and just plain campers wanting to get deeper into nature. A lone single engine airplane painted white and red sat on the near side of the landing strip.

Recognizing the plane's identification numbers on its side, Ian announced, "That's Jeff's, we can fly out after he gets back from the hunt."

Then there it was; they had made it at last. The huge and golden logs of old growth timbers used in its construction never ceased to amaze Jessa as she looked up once again and admired it all. The southern end of the massive structure sported the large windows of the restaurant. Mid section were the steps to the veranda and double door entry at left. To the far right an outside staircase climbed to the family rooms and adjacent balcony that had another staircase, this one spiraling down to the basement's banquet hall.

Reining in and dismounting the two riders were of one mind, though neither one would admit it comforts of civilization were at the top of their lists.

Tying their horses to the hitching post and unpacking their belongings while being careful not to stretch, slump or complain the two walked past the polished white crew cab pickup presenting a magnetic sign on its side stating "Fuller Ranch, Safari & Resort". This was their 'town car'.

Jessa knew that behind the lodge itself and across the river were the bunkhouses for the ranch help and more private cabins for rent. From personal experience she recalled the honeymooners cottage, which she and Grant had rented before their own home was completed and the weather had become too nasty to stay in their tent.

The two weary travelers were at the steps now and Jessa's feet seemed to be lifting cement blocks as she climbed the five wooden steps to the porch, and then dragged them behind Ian to the large wooden double doors that had axes for handles.

Ian reached to open the right side door when out flung the left. It was Frank, the ranch's foreman and right hand man to Josef when Ian was away.

"Hey there, boss!" We missed you last night. Everything all right in the south patch?" He inquired of Ian with a friendly thin-lipped smile while giving a sideways glance and nod to Jessa. Frank was thin all over yet surprisingly strong and enduring for a man in his sixties, and Ian had great respect for Frank's energy and abilities. The older man seemed to have a sixth sense in finding stray livestock, and an uncanny aim when roping dodging animals from the back of a speeding horse, jeep, or motorcycle.

Ian gave the foreman a quick report then added, "Before you head out to move the northeastern stock, Frank, I want you to take these three (and he motioned to the hitching post) to the stables. Grain them and store Mrs. Franklin's tack with our dude string equipment. We will be using them for a time while she is away. I also want you to pick a man to visit her place every couple of days. She has some livestock there that need feeding and it will familiarize the new hands with that end of the ranch. Alright?" He asked.

"Gotcha boss!" And Frank turned to head down the steps.

As the two dogs came trotting from under the outdoor stairs where Bonnie's water and food could be found, and both of them were licking their lips, Ian caught Frank's attention once more.

"Yeah?" The foreman answered him.

"Use 'Big J', and take Bonnie with you. She'll be a good help." And looking at Jessa now Ian continued, "Something has come up and I won't be around for a while."

Hesitantly now Frank responded. "Well, sure Ian, if that's what you want." And his surprise fell upon Jessa's shoulders.

"It is." Ian answered his friend's concern.

Frank called to Bonnie and strode purposefully to the hitching post where he untied the horses, tied Samyra's reins to the saddle horn and landed lightly in 'Big J's saddle. The group of them trotted toward the stables on the far side of the airstrip, Bonnie looking back only once then on to business as usual.

For a few moments the two on the porch and Bozeman on the gravel lot watched them go. Then each let out a sigh and turned to their destiny. Ian opened a door for Jessa to enter the lodge. Taking a deep breath, she stepped inside and Ian closed the door behind them.

Bozeman watched his mistress disappear inside, then looked once more in the direction Bonnie had gone in time to see her disappear into the stables following Rory's bouncing butt. Boze then turned to walk dejectedly to the end of the lodge and flop down under the stairwell, for he had faith the food bowl would once again be filled.

CHAPTER SIX

THE NEWS

"Deep breath now, kiddo." Ian advised Jessa as he released the axe- handle doorknob and they stepped inside the lodge.

Heavy with apprehension Jessa stepped inside the foyer to once again gaze upon the many animal skins and heads adorning the walls of the lodge. Antelope and deer, cougar and fox, coyote and wolf, a large moose head hung solemnly from above the restaurant entry. Years ago, there had been a bearskin rug, until Kent had been killed and it was immediately removed by the staff for the sake of the family.

Setting down his load of camping leftovers and Jessa's duffle bag, (she carried her husband's guitar) Ian stood at the front desk and banged on the bell there. "Anyone work here?" He bellowed humorously and allowed his saddlebags to slip to the floor.

"They're here!" A high-pitched squeal came from the empty restaurant followed by the sound of high heels running across hardwood flooring.

Careening around the corner as a baseball player sliding to home skidded Lorene in an energetic yellow satin frenzy, with bare arms opening wide yet dodging her brother to engulf her "Jessi girl!" Guitar case and all, with oodles and boodles of bubbly giggles and silly laughter, that washed away and evaporated her dear old friend's apprehensions of only a few short moments ago.

Turning his smiling face from the two joyful young women,

Ian's sharp ears could detect the much quieter and more dignified approach of his mother, to whom he went for a warm hug.

"We were starting to wonder dear, thank you for calling in this morning."

"It was necessary, mom. Has there been any word for Jessa?" He asked quietly and searched her eyes, "Yes," proclaimed their deep brown depths, and his arms slid from around her, unsure of what to do next.

But Evelyn Fuller had not become the stouthearted legacy to the family name through indecision and faintness. She was not cold hearted but would not shirk a task at hand, not even that of telling a difficult truth. Instinct told her that her son was not prepared for this, and Lorene did not as yet know, after all, was it necessary for her daughter to be moping about and tearful for her friend's arrival?

"Let's all go to the lounge, shall we?" And asking Ian to please not leave the duffle and saddlebags at the front desk, Evelyn led the three young people through the restaurant that she and her daughter had been decorating a few minutes ago.

Jessa noticed Dr. Edwards sitting at a table across from a man slumped in his chair, she felt she knew him but her mind was focused elsewhere.

Dr. Edwards' gaze shifted to the group heading for the lounge. He had watched last night's news from his resident's cabin and sympathy welled up inside him as his doctor's mind traveled dutifully to case scenarios and supplies on hand, then snapped back to his present patient and their travel plans.

"Please sit down." Evelyn motioned for Jessa and Lorene to sit on the couch. Ian dropped their baggage and stood next to his mother, waiting.

Evelyn chose her words to be as gentle as they could be but their awful meaning could not be softened or mistaken.

Catching Ian's eye, Jessa lost her moment of relief that seeing Lorene had afforded her. Apprehension stiffened her.

Even Lorene stopped chatting long enough to notice that her mother had not sat down.

Evelyn breathed deep and began to explain. "Last night after everyone had gone to bed, as we try to do every evening, Mr. Fuller and I sat together right where you are now and talked about our day, then turned on the news." And she pointed to the television on the wall. "There was an article regarding your husband's outfit in China. Jessa, there was an earthquake centered under the mountain they were stationed on. A landslide took half the village under it, and the team that was on it. No survivors have been found," and in her own words she added for cushion "as yet."

With a long intake of breath Lorene's stilled voice found itself again. "Mother! Why didn't you tell me...?" But mother's hand went up to still her daughter's protest.

"Jessa dear, please let us help you in any way we can." Evelyn continued. "If you need help with your place, a job, lawyer or funeral arrangements, please let us...let me know. I have been where you are right now, and I know it seems like life is over, but be stronger than you have ever been, that is the only way it will get better. Please hang on to that, it will get better."

Ian's attention was stolen away from Jessa by his mother's words and his painful memories of loss mingled with hers. His arm found his mother's shoulders and his eyes rested on her now silver hair, swept back and pinned in a high bun. When had it turned from champagne blonde? He could not remember it happening, for in his mind's eye she remained young and beautiful.

In every creature is instilled the ability and instinct for survival to fight or to flee when crisis happens. Jessa's mind snapped as her unconscious self chose the latter. "Nooo!" She heard her voice ring in her ears as her body flung itself from her seat to dodge hands meant to stop her, and ran to the foyer and outside. She cared not for any thing or any person who may have been on the other side of the doors she burst through, only for escape. Voices called after her, high heels and boots followed her, but she did not care as her own legs flew down the steps and across the graveled parking lot with arms pumping hard toward the stables and away from this awful reality.

Lorene had lunged for Jessa but too late, and now was cursing her blatant choice in footwear as she tripped down the outside steps, and would have fallen onto the gravel had not her brother caught her in mid air and set her back on her feet before taking off after Jessa, his long strides devouring the distance to the stables.

For a moment Lorene stood dumbfounded. She expected to be the only one chasing after her friend, yet there ran Ian, totally out of character and running after Jessa. Lorene mused as she jogged along in her heels and hiked up gown, blonde curls bouncing from the bun atop her head. She stopped to lean against the doorframe of the stable and catch her breath. "Whew! Having a baby certainly changes things!" She gasped, and then spotting Ian searching the stalls at the end of the building for their runaway friend, she trotted toward him.

Ian looked into the last stall and at about the tenth horse he had spooked since racing into the stable, before climbing frantically up the wooden ladder that was nailed to the floor of the hayloft, while calling out "Jessa, please stop and talk to me!" His eyes darted to the wall that held the hay hooks and pitchforks, quickly checking- yes, all accounted for, thank God. He did not know if she would try to harm herself, he prayed not, but he had never seen her this way and did not know. He continued. "You know I will help you any way I can." Only stacks of baled oat and alfalfa hay and straw answered him back, but she _had_ to be here somewhere!

"Jessa, I'm your friend! You need me right now more than ever, and I'm here for you! I won't let you go through this alone; you are not alone anymore! Those days are gone and whatever really did happen to Grant we will find out together and work through it together, alright sweetheart?" Ian was surprised to hear his choice of word. He had not used sweetheart like that since, well, a very long time. He turned at a sound behind him and saw Lorene on the ladder staring at him. She had heard. A faint smile played at her lips. Then they both heard it, uncontrollable sobbing coming from, there! Ian ran up a stack of straw in the midst of the room, grabbing at bales to toss them aside and reveal a hole, spacious enough for this seemingly small child, Jessa, crying like an orphaned waif in the night, curled into a fetal position, hopeless and helpless and barely even conscious.

"Oh dear God." Ian cried as he scooped her up, held her and rocked her until she fainted away in a pool of tears, his mingled with her own.

Lorene called from below. "She is breathing, right?"

"Uh- huh" Was all her brother could answer.

"Well, let's get her into a bed where 'Doc' can see her. I'll go down the ladder first so I can help you bring her down." And Lorene steadied Ian as he climbed oh so carefully down the ladder with Jessa slung over his shoulder. Then he carried her in his arms back to the lodge and to his sister's room.

CHAPTER SEVEN

IN- HOUSE CALL

Lorene trotted up the outside staircase ahead of Ian and opened the door for her brother who carried their friend in his strong arms. "No, Bozeman, you stay outside." She had to tell Jessa's whining dog as she closed the door in his face to trot down the hallway, passing her brother's room and past her brother to open the door of her own room for him.

"You can lay her on my bed and I'll go get Doc." She puffed as she held open her bedroom door for him. "He was in the restaurant with Jeff a few minutes ago."

Ian lay Jessa's limp form onto his sister's canopy bed as Lorene's heels flew down the stairs for help, though she need not have bothered for the moment her yellow satin pump shoes touched the floor Dr. Edwards came purposefully around the corner with his large, cumbersome black physician's bag and a "Now then Lorene, try to calm yourself and tell me what you can about Mrs. Franklin's condition, I saw the news last night myself and have a pretty good idea of what the poor girl is going through, but first hand is always best."

Lorene tried first of all to catch her breath, then somberly recalled the events of the past few minutes as she and 'Doc' climbed the stairs.

Evelyn Fuller had stayed in the restaurant a minute more to assure her few patrons that everything was being done for the woman they all saw being carried back by her son, then she too slipped up the stairs to her daughter's room.

Ian had pulled off Jessa's boots, unbuttoned her jean jacket and was picking hay out of her mass of dark hair when 'Doc' and Lorene entered. Ian brought up a chair for 'Doc' to sit on near the bedside and the older man began to examine this now frail looking woman while listening to the younger man's version of what had happened.

"Yes, I see." 'Doc' would comment to a statement made between listening through stethoscope to his patient's heart, then lungs, and taking blood pressure. He noticed the dried tears on her cheek and gently wiped at them with a cloth as he felt sympathy for her welling up inside him. He sat back and mused for a moment as Mrs. Fuller and her aide, Irene, came in to inspect the scene.

Looking into Mrs. Fuller's eyes 'Doc' told them some of what they knew. "This poor young lady is in mental and emotional shock, compounded by a slow yet steady physical deterioration stemming from stress." And he went on with what they did not expect "If she does not find relief immediately or sooner, there can very well be expected certain character changes. Some minute and barely noticeable, or they may be drastic and irreversible. Now," and 'Doc's gaze switched from Evelyn Fuller to her children "you two seem to be the ones in the know around here about this woman's character, I mean you would be the ones who would first notice any changes in her attitudes, beliefs, that sort of thing?"

In unison Ian and Lorene nodded at 'Doc'.

"Fine, I want you to keep her under close observation for at least forty eight hours and I am going to give her a mild sedative so she can begin right now to get the rest she needs." And 'Doc' took from his bag a pouch which he handed to Irene, saying "Make up a pot of herbal tea for her, and as soon as she wakes up, which I expect will be soon enough with all of us fussing about her, give her a cup with this mixed in. After she rests, <u>make</u> her eat a full meal, there is absolutely nothing to spare on this skeleton of hers! And Lorene, I want you to weigh her on that scale of yours you keep tucked away under this bed, my foot is resting on it that's how I know." And he chuckled at her little secret. "She should come out of this alright with a good support team and that is what we will be. Thank God she made it this far and to this place, otherwise, well enough said." At that, 'Doc' snapped shut his bag and headed back down the stairs, through the foyer and to the restaurant and his first patient of the day, the pilot with the broken foot.

Irene had followed 'Doc' down the stairs, and then she spun to the right on her way to the kitchen to brew the good doctor's potion.

Mrs. Fuller came after her to check with the chef on tonight's menu and its variety. Evelyn wanted Jessa to have her pick of everything they had available. Upstairs Lorene watched over her friend on the bed and sighed, there was nothing she could do for her at the moment and her mother's instincts told her it was time for her baby to wake up. "I need to check on Adam, 'bro', will you be alright?"

"Sure sis, I'll watch her for you. I don't have anything more important to do right now." And Ian took up watch in the chair at the bedside.

Lorene turned to go, then spun back around to give her brother a hug before scooting off to the playpen in the lounge where she found Adam indeed wide awake and playing joyfully with Grandma Dody, who informed the young mother "The next time you need to give someone bad news, you might want to give it somewhere away from a sleeping baby! This poor little tyke shook for a whole half minute before he cut loose balling, and no mother to come and pick him up, on account of she is racing around the ranch after some other crazies, and in her ballroom gown no less!" But then 'Gram's tiny frame shook as she snorted with laughter, for that was how she dealt with life and its many mishaps.

Upstairs in Lorene's room Irene entered with a silver tray, teapot and cup for Jessa. Looking at Ian she asked "Would you like me to watch her for you for a while, if there's something you need to do?"

Ian appreciated the offer but was not sure about not being there when Jessa should awaken. In public Irene would have called him 'sir' or 'Mr. Fuller', although she was the elder of the two by over two decades, but now her gentle voice he had known since childhood called him by name to ease his worry and assure him that Jessa would not be awake for long even if she did come around soon. And Irene, Ian knew, would not leave her side until he or Lorene returned so he left the room to find his mother and dad, as he had a thing to tell them, and a request.

A minute later Ian found his mother in the kitchen conversing with 'Chef' about the moistness of dark meat over light and asked if she and dad could meet with him in the office shortly. Evelyn felt surprise at her son's request and asked, "What, is this a secret? What about Lorene?"

To which he answered her "Well no I guess not, and in fact it might be better if Lorene were to stay on longer than she had planned to."

"Alright Mr. Mystery Man, your dad is doing maintenance on Jessa's Suburban right now, go on out and see if you can persuade him to come in early, you know how he likes tinkering on vehicles."

"I know they are his first love but no competition to you." Smiling broadly Ian yelped as his mother snapped at his behind with a towel.

Outside Ian filled his lungs with the crispness of the day before trotting his long legs to the maintenance shop behind the equipment shed. That moment gave Bozeman a chance to receive a pat and a report on his mistress as Ian comforted the big dog; "Sorry about leaving you out of things, boy, but Jessa needed attention and fast. She will be alright though, so don't you worry, okay?"

The unusually quiet dog licked the man's hand in gratitude for the soothing sound of his voice and the mention of his mistress' name. Bozeman made no attempt to follow Ian, but turned to trot back around the corner and lie down once again under the staircase to wait for Jessa to emerge.

Ian jogged off to find his dad but instead found a note on the shop wall stating "I am off to test my handiwork so don't hold supper on account of me!" A slow smile traveled across Ian's face as he wadded the paper and tossed it to the trash barrel. "Well, dad finally has an excuse to take that rig four wheeling, this could take a while!" And he looked up the old logging road that he and Jessa had ridden in on, little more than an hour ago? So much had happened since crossing the old cattle grate and as he looked up the road Ian could make out a thin wisp of dust on the horizon, his dad would be a while all right. He turned and walked back to the lodge.

Once inside Ian told his mother the contents of his father's note, to which Evelyn replied, "Well, I am willing to venture a guess that your dad will make it home in time to eat with us. He will have his fun getting it all dirty, then his stomach will growl and he will remember our special guest and how 'Chef' does extras for special guests."

"I'm heading back up to Lorene's room mom, I left Irene in charge and you need her back."

"Yes I do. I am nothing without my right arm, and please remind her to bring the tea set back for tonight."

Upon knocking and entering the still open door to the room, Ian saw Jessa turning over to fall back asleep again.

"She's only just taken the tea, Ian." Irene told him. "But the poor dear was so out of it she did not ask where anyone was or anything. Like she did not really care, or certainly not enough to argue anyway. She drank the tea and looked around for a moment, yawned and lie back down. She is the best little patient, really."

Ian thought it was odd that Jessa did not ask for anyone or for more information, or want to get up to look for food for that matter. He inquired, "Did 'Doc' say how long she would be out?"

"No, but I am sure it will not be more than a couple of hours, it was a mild sedative he handed me, though she must be exhausted from worry." Irene took a thoughtful pause before venturing more. "Ian, when my Alex was so ill before he died, I would try to hide it but at times my fear would get the better of me. There would be days when I found myself standing in the middle of a room unable to make any decision of what I should do next. The burden of responsibility was too great. What if I did the wrong thing? Or gave the wrong medicine at the wrong time? Fear paralyzed me at times, if it wasn't for my faith I would never have survived his passing. I don't know your friend very well, but I have seen strength in her. I do know that what 'Doc' said about watching for change in her personality is quite real, having been there I know. For the first three months after his death I was completely lost and incapacitated, and for all of a year the tears flowed over. When people came to call I would muster a false face, one of confidence and durability, until they would leave and the tears could be denied no longer. Since then I was quite freakishly dry of emotion and rarely felt anything could warrant grief enough for a misty eyed concern, until your brother was taken. Oh, if only it could have been me instead, I prayed. But I digress. What I am trying to get at is this. For a long time my soul wondered why Alex could not simply jump out of bed and do all the wonderful things we did together. Eventually it sank in that he could not, and would never again. For Jessa, she has had to wonder about her husband, why doesn't he come? Now she knows why, he cannot. What she intends to do with this new information, this new clarity, is up to her. What she decides may change her and she may not even notice. Be patient if you can for it may prove to be a bumpy ride. Well, I had better get downstairs, I will see you at dinner." Irene picked up the teapot and tray before stepping out of the room.

CHAPTER EIGHT

A DIFFERENT KIND OF DREAM

Ian stirred from his doze in the hard wooden chair by Jessa's bedside when Lorene breezed in with little Adam in her arms. He felt stiff but stood eagerly to hold his baby nephew and kiss the playful toddler's forehead. Adam clamped onto his uncle's forefinger and tried to pull it to his mouth, cooing and slobbering all the while.

Lorene stood over Jessa for a moment, then sat with one hand on her friend's shoulder and spoke to her as if she were conscious and alert. "Okay my Jessi, it will be time to wake up soon and take a nice hot bath. I know how you love to use my scented oils so I brought plenty, and I want to trim your split ends after we shampoo and crème rinse these nasty bad rats' nests out. Then we will dress you up nice and pretty enough so that the men's mouths will drop. I want to try some new makeup on you and I think it will be even more fun if you are awake! Jessi girlfriend, wake up, please? Well in another five minutes then, okay?" And Lorene looked up at Ian apologetically for not being able to rouse their friend.

"I know sis, it's hard to wait. Say, there's something I have to talk to you and the folks about." Ian began.

"I'll say!" Lorene responded. "Ian, I have never in my life been so surprised by you as I am today!"

"I know sis, I feel the same way. I mean I find myself saying and doing things that haven't been planned out first. I plan on riding fence and then realize I am miles from the last unchecked section, because that piece of wire and post doesn't come near her place. I plan on sitting down and holding her hand while talking her quietly and calmly through the most difficult time in her life, and wind up on this frantic chase across the property!"

Wide-eyed Lorene could contain herself no longer. "You do love her don't you?"

Ian's mouth snapped shut, afraid to spill more. Then feeling a warm moisture and a rather brown smell coming from Adam's pants, he handed the little dear over to his mother who took him readily to the changing table at the foot of her bed for a quick clean up.

"I love her the way you love her, sis. She is my friend too."

"Well 'bro', the way I love her is openly and honestly, this means that if I want to see her, then I go straight on over, not in circles first. I think you are kidding yourself."

Dumbfounded, Ian stood speechless for a moment more, and then hung his head in agreement. "What can I do?" He asked helplessly.

"Look," Lorene tried " you know she would be my first choice as a sister in law, but she is totally wrapped up in Grant, and not just now but it has always been that way. I mean, she left her family and home that she loved, to move hundreds of miles away and into another country on basically a whim of his, only to be left home alone half of the time with nobody around for company. I liked Grant and all, but it would drive me stark raving mad to be in love with someone who could overlook me like that. And I guess that's my point. Her love for him is so strong that it has enabled her to live like this, and it is not something that is simply going to go away, even though he has." She paused before quietly adding, "I love you and I don't want to see you hurt again, and that is all I can see happening here. Ian, you have come so far since Kathryn, please don't throw that away." And with that Lorene handed Adam back over to his uncle with, "I believe you two are scheduled for the next shower?"

Ian reached out to the spluttering boy with "Okay mommy, we boys will go clean up our act, I know I can use the diversion!"

And a red faced, thoughtful uncle and his joyous baby nephew discovered together the elation and mystery of a steam filled bathroom.

Left to her own devices Lorene went poking through the duffle bag that a ranch hand had brought up from the lounge, stating "The missus didn't like it left there for people to trip over, ya know?"

To her dismay, Lorene found what she was looking for and sent Jessa's old flowered dress hurtling down the laundry chute. Opening wide her own cache of dresses in her closet, Lorene withdrew a tiny, shimmering black, spaghetti strapped little number that try as she might she simply could not get her postpartum tummy back into, not the way that it should anyway. She had brought the dress back home with her with the intent of giving it to Jessa, only to find that her friend had become an emaciated catwalk manikin. "It won't drape the way it was meant to, but oh well it still beats out the doily dress any day!" Lorene told herself, and proceeded to pick out her choices of colors for Jessa's makeup.

Looking down at her friend sleeping so soundly Lorene decided to make a quick trip to the linen closet down the hall.

If she only had a clue to the workings in her friend's head she would have shaken Jessa to waken her immediately.

Within her dreaming mind Jessa heard her own voice announce "I love you too Ian, and I want us to be together always." She kissed him and they began their walk down the aisle together, arm in arm. It was foggy in the church, but there was enough light to see their family and friends. On her left were her parents and friends, including her beautiful dog, all washed and looking cleaner than she had ever seen him. His ears were up as he watched her come nearer. On Ian's right were his parents and Lorene holding her baby. Next to them were Kent and a lovely young woman with flowers in her long brown hair that matched her robe. She held a lead rope that led to 'Big J's halter, he held his proud head high and whinnied to Ian who laughed aloud and happily.

They came near the altar now, but as the thick mist cleared

there was no minister, but an open casket. Suddenly Grant's tuxedoed corpse sat straight up and with outstretched arm pointed a decaying finger at her, screeching "Jessa! What do you think you are doing? I'm still alive! <u>Alive</u>!"

Screaming at the top of her lungs she dropped Ian's arm and kept on screaming until she collapsed into a dead faint.

Jessa sat bolt upright on the bed, screaming for all she was worth until her breath ran out, then having to stop long enough to inhale gave her time to form the words "I'm sorry! Grant I am so sorry, I didn't mean to!"

Lorene was in the doorway staring at Jessa when Ian burst out of the bathroom, clenching a towel around his waist with one hand and holding a slippery Adam with the other, whom he handed over to Lorene before stepping cautiously toward Jessa, who did not seem to notice the three of them for she was staring forward at no one at all and breathing fast. Blinking, her wide eyes seemed to refocus, allowing reality to seep in around her horrific vision.

From somewhere outside a big dog barked then howled.

Slowly Ian stepped forward, cautiously, unsure.

Jessa's face was filled with confusion until momentarily she remembered where she was and whom these people were and that this was reality, not that other scene.

A tear rolled down her flushed face to be wiped away by Ian's comforting hand, and for a moment she allowed herself to be held before the memory of Grant's accusation in her tortured mind made her force him away. "No! I can't!" Was all she could say.

Ian lowered his arms. Studying her he asked, "Jessa, was this time different than the others?"

Lorene breathed the word "Others?"

"Yeah, sis. Jessa has been having nightmares about Grant."

"And you would know this, how?" Lorene asked her brother.

"Because she told me, okay?"

"Well," Lorene mused, "I guess I don't know everything, yet."

Ian's eyes had never left Jessa's, and now she answered his question with a gulp, "Uh huh." At his urging she continued. "He, he accused me of, of forgetting about him." She would say no more about it and looked away.

Lorene broke into the ensuing silence, "Well uncle Ian is leaving a nice puddle on our floor, isn't he Adam?"

Ian realized he was wearing a wet towel which he nearly lost control of when his sister gently tossed her toddler into his unready arms, with a sinister giggle.

"I believe you two have some secret rendezvous? Something about an uncle's secret? Scat! Shoo!" And once again a red faced gentle giant left the room with his rosy-cheeked nephew.

After some quick explaining at the foot of the stairs to the small crowd that had gathered below, "I thought I saw a mouse but it turned out to be my brother's sock in the hallway!" And at her laughter all went back to their business of entertainment while shaking their heads at the flightiness of a young woman. But Lorene did not care, for curiosity had been satisfied.

Returning to a relieved and grateful Jessa, Lorene helped her friend get up and gather a few necessaries for her bath. "I want you to take a shower first to get the top layer of dirt off, sorry to be so blunt, kiddo. <u>Then</u> you can melt into a hot oil bath and I will trim off the bottom inches of split ends.

The two young women were unusually quiet during most of the grooming process, when ordinarily they would chat each other up about all topics under the sun with giggles being the main course. Lorene tried to maintain a light and airy attitude for the sake of her friend, it was not how she felt however, as she filed and painted Jessa's nails before rinsing and combing her raven tresses to pile them high atop her head. The scented oils and hot water created a sweet flower garden sauna.

A soft knock came at the door and Lorene got up from her stool to open it ever so slightly, so as not to spoil Jessa's privacy. Standing back away from the door now was "Ah! Is this some James Bond character with a midget partner? No, it's everyone's favorite hunky actor accepting his Oscar! You two look so adorable! Ian you truly are the most wonderful brother!" She kissed his cheek, "Let me show Jessa how cute Adam looks!" And Lorene lifted her son with both arms full of hugs and kisses for him for which he squealed in delight.

"Adam, you are the most precious little thing I have ever seen!" Jessa exclaimed. "Where on earth did Ian find a tuxedo to fit him?" She asked.

"I don't know." Lorene said while shaking her head slowly in fond amazement. "But wait until you see him. I knew he was cooking up something but I had no idea it would be this special! I will have to put in a good word for him come Christmas time." She giggled and handed her son back out to Ian who had waited patiently in the hallway, pleased with the attention Adam was receiving, and a little envious of it. "Of course you realize it will be a while before we ladies will be ready." Lorene whispered to her brother. "Adam loves to play with the piano keys, you two could duet it a little while longer, right?" Then tongue in cheek to him, Lorene finished with "I promise it will be worth the wait."

Without a word to Lorene, Ian turned with Adam, saying to the toddler "Let's play piano!" and "Whee!" All the way down the stairs with Adam bouncing gaily on his uncle's shoulder.

Lorene closed the bathroom door once more, and with a sigh she said to herself, "If only he could find the right one, he would be such an awesome father."

"What did you say?" Jessa queried over the sound of dribbling water.

"Hmm? Oh! Nothing really. Well let's get you out and dressed so we can set and dry, makeup and eat! Chasing you around has been more running than I have done in a long while, and I'm hungry so you must be starved!"

And in fact Jessa felt a little woozy as she stood up from the tub. She had not had but an old pear all day, very little the day before, and for a moment the room seemed to spin.

As Lorene handed Jessa a towel to dry off with, it struck her like a slap how skinny her friend had become, something she used to think would be pretty cool to be, although now she was not so sure as she viewed the many ribs poking through tight skin, and hip bones in plain view with nothing to provide cover for the imagination. What would Grant have thought had he known?

"Sweetie, doctor Edwards wants to update his chart on you since you are here, help me humor him and stand on the scale, alright? Thanks, hon. Whoa! One hundred eighteen pounds! Girlfriend, did you <u>know</u> you had lost twelve pounds?"

Hesitantly Jessa replied "I, well I guess I knew my jeans have been loose for some time, but I don't keep a scale."

"Alright that does it, let's hurry things up a bit." And they hurried their business in the bathroom, then the finishing touches in Lorene's room, and finally Lorene was satisfied with her work and they could join the family downstairs.

Lorene led the way with her long yellow gown swish swishing as she held the banister with her right hand and a fold of her dress in the left. Appearing every inch a princess with her long golden hair piled high and bouncing in ringlets down the sides of her face, Lorene accepted her baby prince graciously from Ian and carried him to his highchair at the royal family's banqueting table.

Following princess Lorene came her starlet friend, taking slow gentle steps in black high-heeled strap sandals holding each delicate ankle. Jessa was not used to such footwear and missed her wide heeled boots, until she saw Ian and her ruby lips parted in awe. She blinked, but it was real, this handsome vision. She could not help but say "Oh, wow." under her breath, and yet it was more than he could muster, for as Lorene had predicted his mouth had dropped and lay quite useless.

Ian held out his arm for Jessa to take when her feet touched the floor, and for a moment only she hesitated, then took it and together they walked arm in arm to dinner.

CHAPTER NINE

CLARITY

Ian led Jessa through the foyer and into the restaurant. Turning right they strolled across the shining hardwood floor to the long table where the family would eat. The room was dimly lit by candles at their table and also on the smaller round tables that lined the perimeter of the room at the windows. There were a few customers at the smaller tables but hardly more than what were seated at the Fuller's long family table.

Jessa smiled at Grandma Dody and nodded to Doctor Edwards who sat at the end and at Dody's right hand. At 'Gram's left were her great grandson Adam in his highchair and bib, and his mother who sat next to her mother, and at the head of the table was Josef with Ian to his left. On Jessa's left and between her and 'Doc' was the pilot she had seen earlier but had not readily recognized, as she was used to seeing him standing or sitting quite straight and uprightly.

Tonight however, Jeff sat slumped in his chair. His eyes were at half-mast, as he looked her up and down, slurring a greeting with a half smile thrown her way. "You look _really_ good thish evening Mishus Franklin! If I had two good legs I would ask for a dance!"

"I dance with my husband." Jessa returned her chilly answer.

"Ouch, I didn't mean anything by it." He pouted.

Lorene jumped to the pilot's rescue with "Well Jeff, still not wasting any time before sticking your foot in your mouth, I see." And she flashed him a bright smile to say "It was okay".

"Yeah, I guess there's no hope for me, 'specially when 'Doc' here is so eager to keep me doped up on pain killers." Jeff offered as an apology.

"So what happened to you this time?" Ian wanted to know.

"Oh, man…" Jeff's cracking voice began "I've flown across mountains in hail storms, over lakes in blizzards and plains in a dust cloud, had my picture in the paper the day I delivered serum to stop an outbreak of Asian flu, I've never had a problem with my equilibrium. So why can't I <u>drive</u> without rolling over?" He snorted with laughter until the pain registered in his brain, "OW! Ow don't make me laugh, please don't make me laugh, I bruised my ribs." Jeff sighed before continuing "I was driving a quad on the edge of this little ole' creek bank, with my rifle on back and looking out for grizzly, when I heard something rustling about in the brush. It was a <u>big</u> something and I spun around to reach for my rifle when the whole embankment gave way and over I went with the quad landing on top of my legs!" He grimaced at the memory. "I yelled for what seemed like hours before my partner showed up. I couldn't reach the two-way, and it had been munched anyway. This is my sixth roll over since I got my license, maybe they'll take it away." And his red eyes stared at the empty table.

Evelyn asked Josef to say grace before they ate.

"Now, just because I'm going to hold my wife's hand doesn't mean that any of you have to hold hands, especially you Jeff!" And Josef snickered under his breath before asking them to bow their heads. "Dear Lord," He began "thank you for protecting us this day, otherwise we might not have made it to this bountiful feast before us. Thank you for the many blessings you have bestowed upon us, Father. Tonight we especially ask you to send your holy comforter to one here today that is missing her beloved husband. Please guide her now and give her strength to carry on, in Jesus' precious name, amen."

And as Josef opened his eyes he met Jessa's own grateful, misty-eyed gaze.

"You're welcome." He quietly told her with a wink as

everyone else poured out conversation on their way (except Jeff) to the buffet.

Once again Jessa clung to Ian's arm, as much for support as for company or convention. Finally at the buffet she scooped up a plate and began choosing from mountains of food. There was potato salad, leafy greens with roasted garlic croutons, freshly sliced pineapple and peaches, mashed potatoes with brown gravy and breads aplenty with whipped honey butter and apricot marmalade. Jessa heaped these onto her plate, leaving the carved turkey, barbecued chicken and roasted beef to the others. When asked why she merely stated between bites "When it's not necessary I don't eat meat, and besides, what I have really been missing is right here."

Irene brought a full plate to Jeff, who thanked her profusely and asked for a rain check on a dance. No one except 'Gram' seemed to notice that Irene darted a glance to 'Doc' at that moment, before gracefully bowing out of the invitation and excusing herself to return a quarter of an hour later with a dessert cart full of slices of pies and small bowls of ice cream, others with tapioca pudding.

Jessa had slowed considerably with her chewing and swallowing by this time, and a warm cozy feeling filled her stomach that she had not known for a very long time. Being close to the round fireplace in the middle of the room it was quite warm even without a jacket, and for a moment she thought about taking another nap.

"Care for a slice of pie?" Irene inquired from over Jessa's shoulder while gesturing to the dessert cart.

"Oh my, dessert. I think I have run out of room Irene, but thank...is that rhubarb pie? Well yes, I'll take that thinner slice please, thank you!" And Jessa proceeded to indulge.

Ian chose a small bowl of pineapple sherbet.

"Mm...oh, this is sooo good!" Jessa moaned in delight.

Ian's spoon stopped dead short of his mouth. Slowly his head turned toward her, watching as she took another forkful of the tart yet sweetly spiced pie.

"Ian dear," His mother prompted from across the table "You are about to drip sherbet on your new suit."

Lorene tried not to choke but it was too late, her mother patted her on the back and offered Lorene her water glass for a sip.

"Goodness! Haven't I taught you to chew thoroughly?" Evelyn demanded lightly. "Okay now? Good. Let's not frighten Adam anymore, shall we?" For her grandson was blinking at his mother as if he might cry.

Evelyn noted that Karen had entered the room to begin the evening's music. The slim young woman wore her long blonde hair straight and loose down her back, framing her face and gentle blue eyes. Her lithe body was clad in a long flowered dress with short loose sleeves for freedom of movement as she glided across the room to the black baby grand piano and began playing softly at first, unnoticeably to those in deep conversation. Her lilting voice sang a ballad of old, a song of love lost upon the ocean waves, ending in an enchantment of trills and peaking notes that faded with the sea mists.

Amid rapturous applause Karen stood and bowed to her meager audience before introducing herself and asking for requests. She received many that night as she did every time she played.

Jessa sat enraptured by the wonderful workings of the ivory keys and the crystal clear voice of the songbird. Her pie now gone but not forgotten, she almost dreaded the sight of Irene returning with a second cart, this one contained coffee, tea, sodas and hot apple cider, which she chose in a tall glass with a long cinnamon stick, saying "<u>Thank</u> you Irene! Please tell me you will not bring out anymore carts." She begged with a smiling grimace while holding her tummy with one hand.

"Then my mission is accomplished." Irene smiled and winked at Jessa as she excused herself to offer delights to the rest of the guests.

Evelyn and Josef excused themselves to the dance floor and were soon joined by other couples. The floor was far from capacity and the couples had more than enough room to spread out, and yet they felt friendship and talked amongst themselves gaily in a tightly knit grouping.

"'Doc', take me for a spin!" An elegant in black lace Dody invited her old friend as she grabbed him by the hand and led him to the dance floor.

Of the five left at the table, one had a broken foot, one was learning to walk, one was wishing she had not been wearing her pumps all day, one was wishing he could take her to the dance floor while he knew she would not allow it, and she sat next to him praying he would not ask.

"Hey Ian, be a buddy and get me to the restroom?" Jeff broke the silence. "'Doc' helped me about four hours ago, then it was time for guzzling water with pills, and, y' know?"

"Sure, Jeff. Ladies, please excuse us." Ian helped Jeff up and onto his crutches before the two men disappeared around the corner.

"You used to date him didn't you?" Jessa remembered.

"Strange, isn't it? Funny how it seemed like a good idea at the time." Lorene admitted. "I mean, he's tall and blonde like a god, has curls like Custer and is fun loving, and usually can say what a lady wants to hear, it's an instinct with him I guess. But he has no idea what commitment is about, or _for_, even."

"I'm glad you found Dave, hon." Jessa reported with a snicker.

Frowning, Lorene replied "Yeah, me too. Are you all right? I mean, you seem rather carefree, considering."

A cloud shadowed Jessa's countenance as she answered boldly, "Grant is not dead!" And she stood up, left the table and sauntered over to the piano. Karen was finishing an instrumental before taking a break and the two women struck up a conversation.

Lorene shook her head and stood to get Adam out of the highchair. When she picked him up to go to bed, Lorene spotted Ian and Jeff coming slowly from the restroom and she walked over to them.

From the piano and her conversation with Karen, Jessa noticed Lorene talking with Ian, who looked her way momentarily before he and Jeff headed for the lounge.

"Thanks man, you're a good friend." Jeff said to Ian while reaching out to pat him on the back and nearly falling over.

"So it is true. A friend in need is a friend indeed." Ian replied.

"I hope you're not trying to make me laugh." Jeff retorted.

"Sorry. Here, my folks will probably want to check the news before turning in but other than that you are King of the remote". Ian told his friend as he handed him a pillow and a blanket.

Jeff got comfortable on the couch and yawned, "Thanks for offering your room but those stairs are way too scary right now, g'night." And immediately he drifted off to sleep.

Ian stood over him for a few seconds, half believing Jeff was fooling around as usual, but no, he really was sleeping. "Huh, it must be nice to be able to do that." Ian said quietly to himself as he left the lounge in search of Jessa, whom he found in Karen's company. The two women were tinkering with a duet. He stopped and listened. Ian was familiar with Karen's singing voice, but could not remember Jessa ever breaking into song in his presence, although Grant had. "Gee, they compliment each other well don't they 'Gram'?" Ian asked of Dody when she and 'Doc' sailed over from the dance floor, and 'Gram', being winded from the lively little ditty played, had to catch her breath before giving her approval of the ladies' performance. Then she noticed Irene looking wistfully toward them and whisked 'Doc' away again, for she knew he would never have conceived of such a plan for himself, to make Irene jealous enough to make her move, and 'Gram' felt that these two should be together. Her plan was working.

Evelyn and Josef left the dance floor and said their goodnights to friends and family as they made their way to the lounge. Ian stood behind Karen and Jessa to listen intently. "Beautiful." He decided then bent low to ask, "Jessa, would you like to use the phone now?"

"In a minute." She answered without looking away from Karen until the end of the tune, and obviously enjoying herself with one of the few people around who did not know of her husband's plight and so did not mention it, allowing her to relax.

Jessa thanked Karen for the interlude then excused herself to walk with Ian out of the restaurant and into the foyer. "This phone?" She asked at the front desk.

"Actually I thought that you might prefer the privacy of the den." And he gestured for her to follow him through the door found tucked away under the staircase. They entered and Ian closed the door. The room was cold, being far away from the fire and the furnace had long since been turned off for the night.

Ian lifted the handset and held it out for Jessa to take after he pushed a button to dial out of the complex. "Otherwise your conversation can be heard all over the compound." He cautioned. "It's cold in here, wouldn't you be warmer with your hair down? I know how." And he deftly pulled hairpins out of her 'do', allowing the captured raven locks to fall about her bare shoulders. Jessa shivered, but not from the cold. "I'll be right back." And he left her standing there holding the phone, and breathing.

Slowly and painfully she dialed the area code to her in-laws'.

CHAPTER TEN

"NO ESTAN EN CASA"

Dial tone, beeping, ringing, answering. "Hola, este` es Jorge`, habla` espanol?

Surprised, Jessa stammered. "Este` es Jessa Franklin, Yo tengo un poco espanol. Donde estan los senores Franklin por favor?"

A pause, "Los padres de su esposo no estan en casa, hondalay rapido con ADRA." He supplied.

"ADRA? Jorge, me comprende? Adventist Development y Relief Agency?"

"Si, si. ADRA, si!" He responded happily at their ability to communicate.

Jessa tried again. "Jorge`, a donde` fueron los senores Franklin con ADRA?"

"China."

Jessa nearly fell onto the desk. "China?" She asked incredulously, her voice cracking, not noticing that Ian had stepped into the room to place a black velvet jacket around her cold trembling shoulders.

"Si, si. Sus padre y madre de tu esposo en China con ADRA, okay?"

Dejectedly she answered back, "Okay, si, gracias. Adios Jorge." A stunned Jessa lowered the receiver, but forgot what to do with it next as she stood there leaning on the desk for support.

Ian cleared his throat and took the receiver from her hand to put it back in its holster. "I didn't know you spoke Spanish."

Preoccupied she responded. "I don't, really. I picked up a little in Mexico when Grant's team was on assignment there. Mostly I went shopping and toured with a couple of the other part time wives." She used the term disgustedly. "Right now I wish I had another chance to sit idly by and watch him drill holes through rock, or spending hours making sense of his computer generated, three dimensional holographic maps, anything. Do you know that someday we won't need cars or airplanes, trains or buses? We will simply 'void' from point A to point B. No, really it's true. I have seen it. In testing of course, but it is possible. Grant is that kind of genius. He is above our plane of thinking. He can think outside the box that most people confine themselves in by using one simple word, impossible. Grant doesn't use that word.

"Jessa, did you ask when they would be back?" Ian inquired.

"No, I couldn't. I don't know how, because I think inside the box."

And she could say no more without breaking down.

Ian blinked back tears before gaining control enough to assure her she was an intelligent person and worthy of anyone's respect. "Now, in the morning you and I will put our heads and resources together and figure out the best course of action, but right now I need to speak with my folks about taking off for a while, maybe a long time. So, may I escort you to your room for the night before I do that?"

Jessa agreed and they left the den.

Climbing the staircase they came to Lorene's room. The door was ajar and Jessa peeked in to see Lorene and her baby snuggled together under a fluffy comforter. Quietly she reached down to pick up her duffle bag and close the door, and realized that her bag and its contents had been cleaned. "Irene is amazing!" She said to herself.

Ian motioned for her to follow him to his room down the hall. She hesitated for a moment before following.

Jessa had never seen Ian's bedroom door open before, let alone been inside, and now she stood somewhat in awe, for this 'bachelor's pad' was not what one might expect. It had no claim to shame in either cleanliness or decorum. A collection of antique guns adorned one wall; no doubt they were family heirlooms. Then there was the massive redwood bed, and near it stood an artist's easel, containing paints and charcoals in its tray. On one wall a dozen or so framed pictures done in charcoal hung. They were mostly nature scenes, and one of Evelyn and Josef in a happy embrace. There was one large exquisite color hanging of 'Big J', which captured the horse's spirit and love for the artist that kept Jessa's attention for many moments. But resting on the easel the most recent effort was yet to be completed. A large sheet of a woman in jeans, boots and jacket with long black hair flying loose in the wind, in front of her a little bridge, while behind stood a small log cabin and large hairy dog whose attention was fixed on her. Her face was set in confusion as if she did not know which way she should go. Come across the bridge and into the world of the artist? Or return to her cabin to wait? The animated Jessa stood staring at this, embarrassed to be portrayed so, and yet it was darned accurate of him.

"I'm sorry if it makes you uncomfortable." Ian offered in consolation. He was embarrassed to be found out.

"I had no idea you are so well gifted. They are all incredible, Ian."

He smiled warmly at her praise. "Thank you. I'll just grab my sweats from the dresser and head to the den. I hope you sleep well, Jessa."

As he turned to go she replied, "Better than last night on the cold hard ground I am sure. But hey, for as bad a bed as it was, well I want you to know I slept better than I have for a long while. I guess it was because I felt secure and not so alone."

Her grateful smile warmed his heart as Ian forced himself to say "Goodnight" before closing the door behind him.

CHAPTER ELEVEN

"THANKS DAD"

Stopping at the linen closet in the hallway for a woolen blanket before skipping down the stairs with a whistle on his lips, Ian collected his parents from the lounge. They had been quietly watching the news in the chairs opposite Jeff's makeshift bed, with the pilot quietly snoring away.

The three walked through the foyer and into the den, Ian holding the door for his parents.

"Alright son, what is this big secret all about?" Josef wanted to know as he and Evelyn sat on the couch expectantly.

Their son inhaled slowly. "Dad, mom, I don't know for a fact what has happened with Grant, or to him. But I do know Jessa needs help right now, and I am committing myself to her aid <u>right now</u>. I will be leaving for an undetermined amount of time. I assume we will be driving to town with 'Doc' and Jeff in the morning, as of course Jeff is unable to pilot a plane for what, a few weeks anyway?" His parents agreed with the estimate. "From there we should be able to find a flight to Montana or wherever she needs to go. I overheard a bit of her telephone conversation when I came back in here with your velvet jacket for her, mom, and heard the word "China". I don't imagine she and I will be going there, but I want you to know, I will."

His parent's eyes suddenly bulged, brows frowning at first, then arching their shock and surprise while both their mouths had popped in wordless speech.

"Please breathe." Their son prompted them.

At that they both inhaled, smiled, and then laughter tumbled out followed by his mother's tears.

"What?" Their befuddled offspring muttered.

"Son, we are just beside ourselves with relief, is all." Josef began.

"Ian dear, try to understand." Evelyn interjected. "It has been eight years since you have shown us any sign of being able to reach out to another human being this way. I mean aside from your own family and a few choice friends and ranch hands, and dad and I are so happy for you that of course we will support you however we can." Evelyn said while wiping a tear from her cheek.

"Son I'm proud of you, so let's get crackin'!" Josef stood and went purposefully to the front side of his desk to pick out a key, insert it into the bottom filing cabinet drawer and pull out a box containing, "You will be needin' your passport, maybe. And a lot of identification, and the same with money so take these packs (of money) there is our kind and American, and take these credit cards." And Josef shoved several envelopes at Ian until he accepted them all.

"Dad I don't know what to say." And he hugged his father and mother hard and long, not knowing how long it would be before he could embrace them again.

"All ya gotta do is come back safe and sound, son, safe and sound." And in vain Josef tried not to sniffle.

Releasing one another at last, Ian bid his parents a 'goodnight' and they left him to make up his bed on the black leather buttoned couch in the den. It was a tad short for him but much more comfortable than his situation of the night before. He pulled off his shoes then loosened his bowtie and unbuttoned his jacket and shirt to be replaced with a pullover sweatshirt, and then sweatpants replaced dress trousers. Placing his ensemble over a chair Ian was then ready for bed and as was his custom when in private, Ian knelt on bended knees with head bowed to thank his God for an eventful day and for His care therein. He also noted his gratitude for an answer to prayer, in that he was now integrated more closely in Jessa's life, and then Ian asked for a new blessing. "And please continue to be close to us in our journey, Abba, that we may comfort and strengthen, protect and understand each other enough to grow in friendship and caring. And please help us to return home safely, in Jesus' precious name, amen."

Ian rose to his feet and lifted the blanket when he heard a soft voice coming from, outside? He slipped back into his shoes and opened the den door, listened for a moment, then strode through the foyer and the door to the outside. Seeing no one there, he stood on the porch in the chill of the misty night, listening. He crept slowly forward to the end of the porch, not in fear but trying to make no sound to distract his ears from the voice.

"We will be alright, Bozie. You take care of me and I take care of you, just like it's always been. We don't need a bunch of people telling us we don't know what's what, now do we?" And the big dog licked her face all over in gratitude that his mistress had come outside to show him she was alive and well.

Ian stopped just short of the corner of the building; another step and they would be able to see him. Surely Bozeman would have heard his footsteps had the dog not been so enraptured by Jessa's attention.

He felt it a despicable thing to do, but Ian lingered in the dark a full minute longer. He needed to feel assured that Jessa was not planning to escape in secret to hunt for Grant on her own. Once satisfied he then stepped back a few paces and off of the porch onto the gravel parking lot, to approach the end of the building as if he were out for an evening stroll.

"Woof!" Bozeman greeted him but did not leave Jessa's side, who did not rise from her kneeling position, one hand still on her dog. She had reverted back to her blue jeans and boots, wool lined jean jacket and hat, obviously warmer than she had been in the den.

"So?" She asked of him, "Nine o'clock and all's well? You seem to be on patrol. Are you?"

"Nope, just looking around and thought I heard someone. Was it you Bozeman?" And Ian bent low to pet the now blissfully happy dog. "See, Boze, I told you Jessa was okay." And Ian also received a tongue bath.

"Now there is the best thing about a dog." Jessa surmised. "They have enough love, and slobber, to lick anyone who gets close enough over and over again and move on to the next person and start all over, not getting bored with it, or tired. They are not too proud to say I love you, or I need you, or please pet me. Not at all like people are they? Talk about a missing link, to eternal bliss that is. Sometimes when I think about God, I wonder if He has a dog sitting by His throne to pet while He thinks things through." Jessa smiled wistfully then sobered to ask, "Did you speak with your parents?"

"I did, and they could not be more supportive. I will pack in the morning and we can head out after breakfast. Did you want to take your rig?" Ian ventured a guess.

"Wow, you really are coming with me." She thought aloud.

"Yeah, really- really. Didn't you believe me?" He was hurt.

"I thought I did, but now I know it is real, tangible. Not another dream. Thank you. I know that's not enough, but it is all I have to offer right now."

"It is enough Jessa. Anything else is icing on the cake."

She blushed in the moonlight and for the first time, allowed him to see it. "Well, goodnight then. Is bright and early okay? I am feeling the clock ticking again."

"I will wake you before sunup. We will eat and drag Jeff out of bed. He and 'Doc' can breakfast at the hospital. 'Doc' wants x- rays and a better cast for him, and to set up a nurse to visit him at his place. You and I will be long gone by then, sound good?"

"Exactly right, except that I should be the one on the couch, not you. Are you sure I can't change your mind?" She asked in earnest.

"You need your privacy, and dad will be working away in his office by five o'clock. Every morning he comes in here with a cup of hot brew before breakfast to go over notes and figures and start all the hands off on their assignments for the day. They will have a little pow-wow at the breakfast table in case someone has a bright idea or a concern. You and I will be top discussion, I know that."

"Well then yes, to your question. Bozie here fits very well in the back section of the Suburban. He has a mat there between the double doors and the third seat. He curls right up and enjoys sleeping there. In fact he has logged many a contented mile in that spot. We stop every hundred miles or so to stretch our legs at a rest area and have a meal, drink and play a bit before trekking onward. And it has four-wheel drive that can be engaged from the inside. I used to hate having to go out into the weather to push or pull the locking hubs on my dad's old pickup. Hm, sounds like I am tired. I tend to ramble when I get tired. So sleep well, sir Ian." She stood, told Bozeman to stay, and climbed the outside stairs to the bedroom level, opened the door and stepped inside, closing it behind her and leaving Ian and Bozeman staring up after her.

"Well goodnight Bozeman." And the two lowered their heads and went each to his bed, the dog circling before laying down under the stair-case and next to the food bowl, the man walking back across the porch and to the den.

The night stretched out before them, she had pre-travel jitters, he tossed and turned with plans that could not be set. They would have been better off, for sleep that is, in the wilderness laying side by side on the frozen ground.

CHAPTER TWELVE

A LITTLE INFO.

Finally Ian's day began by his father, with steaming cup in hand, carefully knocking and entering the den. It was mint tea he had chosen to warm his bones today while he waited for the furnace to warm the frigid room. "Wake up, son! Do some Jumping Jacks or somethin'! This room needs your body heat. Look at my breath! Brrr!"

And Ian, his eyes not wanting to come open for they had not had their full rest, had trouble remembering why he was scrunched up on the cold couch instead of stretched out in his cozy, rambling bed. Only for a moment, however. Then leaping off of it and into his shoes he demanded of his dad, "What time is it?"

"Coming down on five thirty, you in a hurry or something?"

And the only answer Josef received was his son closing the door behind him.

Josef only smiled and shook his head as he read his notes to himself from the previous day, then left the den to talk with his wife who was in the kitchen with the cook and Irene. He knew the ranch hands would be trickling in soon for breakfast and a short meeting before the day's toil began. Today they would be one hand short, and Josef realized he was already missing his son.

Ian ran up the stairs with his bundle, his feet skipping every other step until lighting on the top floor, then suddenly feeling embarrassed about his enthusiasm he switched to tip toeing down the hall. He knew it was too early for his sister to be up and besides; she was on vacation and also would have been up during the night with Adam to feed and diaper him. He stopped at the linen closet to deposit his borrowed items, then with his suit draped over one arm he stood at his bedroom door, cleared his throat, and knocked softly until Jessa answered as quietly "Yes?"

"It's me, and it's time to get started. Are you ready?"

"I need two minutes." She answered back.

"Perfect. I'll be in the shower that long then we can switch, alright?"

"That's fine." Her sleepy voice answered and yawned as she stretched. Then upon hearing the bathroom door go shut and the shower's water running, Jessa slid out from under the covers to land lightly on the luxuriously soft Lynx fur rug under her feet. Although she still felt clean and pampered from all of the bathing of the previous evening, who knew how things would go? So, switching places with Ian, Jessa also showered briskly while she had the chance, then re packed her toiletries into the duffle bag and hoisted it over a shoulder, stating as she placed her free hand on the door knob "Ready or not."

Upon emerging from the bathroom Jessa met Ian in the hallway. He was closing the door of his room and had a suitcase on wheels in tow with one hand; a backpack slung over one shoulder, and a leather briefcase.

"Are you ready?" He asked.

"I need Grant's guitar." She responded. "It's in Lorene's room, I'll get it." But as Jessa was about to knock the door opened and Lorene's smiling yet sad eyed face greeted her. She was holding the guitar case, which she set down in order to hug Jessa 'goodbye', and squeezed Ian's hand. The two women parted, and the pajama clad Lorene handed over the beloved instrument to her friend, then closed the door and holding a hand over her mouth, cried silently over life's injustices.

The two kept stride together down the stairs, deposited their baggage under the same, and marched with purpose to ensure that 'Doc' and Jeff were also motivating for travel. They were. 'Doc' had given the pilot a pain pill and the two were heading to the restroom.

"Good morning dear, hungry? How about a nice hot plate full of hash browns, eggs and toast?" Evelyn greeted her son, and to Jessa, "Did you sleep well Jessa?"

"Yes thank you. Um, I'm not hungry so I'll take our stuff out while you eat, Ian."

"Jessa," he countered, "Let's have a quick bagel and juice, that won't take long, then we will be on our way, alright?"

"Alright, you are right. I am trying to rush things." She quipped nervously.

They ate quickly and headed with their loads to the Suburban that Josef had already had one of the hands go fetch for them. 'Doc' helped Jeff down the steps and up into a middle seat, then setting his big black bag next to Jeff's crutches he clambered into the rear bench seat so that his patient could stretch out his long legs. Looking behind his seat, 'Doc's eyes met those of Bozeman. The big canine, with ears up, 'woofed' low at him as his hairy tail beat the back of the seat and the back doors.

It had been raining lightly and now it began to pour as Dody and Irene stepped out onto the veranda to wave their goodbyes from under the shelter of the porch roof.

Jessa waved to them while backing the vehicle away from the lodge, then headed out.

The road was wet, muddy and full of potholes as it was late in the year and so it had been months since its last treatment of graveling and grading. This meant that Jessa had to drive more slowly than she wanted to but at least they were finally moving, at last she could search for clues.

A little more than three miles from the lodge they crossed over the last cattle grate and onto a paved road leading to town, where pedal found metal and The Franklin Flyer, as Grant had nicknamed their vehicle, lived up to its name as they soared over the pavement and into town.

Their first stop of course was the hospital. Ian hopped

out and returned with a wheelchair for Jeff, which the pilot maneuvered pretty well considering his medication. Doctor Edwards took over now and with bag and crutches in hand he led his patient to the x-ray lab.

Ian returned to the 'Flyer' and closed the door as Jessa pulled away from the curb. He watched her in silence for several minutes. She rarely blinked and never looked at him, offering no conversation. He wondered if she thought she might drive to China.

The rain calmed a little before turning to slush, it was trying to snow.

Jessa turned up the defroster as the cold air outside caused her windshield to fog up, and as much as she hated to she had to slow down.

Minutes later the 'Flyer' rolled up to the trading post and deposited two people and a dog. The dog stayed outside to sniff the many hundreds of scents left behind by the daily visitors since he had been there last. Some were exciting, canine friends he had made in days gone by, or meats from trapping, and some were curious scents, spices for cooking or scented candles, lamp oils and dried fruits and vegetables. Bozeman reveled in all the sights, sounds and smells of the post while his mistress disappeared inside.

Ian followed Jessa and let the old wooden door swing shut of its own accord, as it had been designed to do. The slamming sound it made alerted the two men in back that customers were afoot.

The younger of the two proprietors emerged first, in his middle seventies he was the son of the slower, (and now shorter) older man in his early nineties. Ian greeted each with a warm smile and nod, for they were like family to him, having been friends of his grandfather's.

"Hello Zeke, how is business?" Ian inquired.

"Good night! If it ain't ole' Ian Fuller!" And the two shook hands.

"Well, they are good and getting better! But maybe this here snow is going to slow things up for a bit." He announced as he peered through a knothole to check the weather. "People forget how to drive an' stuff for a while when the first snow falls. But they will be back for those extra blankets they have been meaning to stock up on an' all. Then before ya know it they will be thinking of all the pretty Christmas trinkets they want for their tots. They'll be back. Gives us a breather, don't it dad?" Zeke asked of his father who had only just joined the group.

"Snow? Did you say snow?" And he cupped an ear for an answer.

"Yeah dad I said snow." Zeke answered him.

Ian raised his voice a bit and offered, "It's good to see you again, Ignacious! You remember Mrs. Franklin here, don't you?"

And the old man beamed at Jessa, his murky blue eyes seeming to sparkle now as he focused on her.

"You know I do, she's my favorite!" Then more seriously as he remembered her age old question "No, sweetie, there's no word from your husband. I have been checkin' my e-mails religiously, but nothing. Not from Grant or his team members even. Just ain't right, is it? But you keep believing he's coming back because I know he is a good man that would never do you wrong. A man would have to be plumb dyin' loco to forget about you! And that feller is real smart, I seen that about him right away, yes sir!" And Ignacious grabbed hold of Jessa's hands for emphasis.

"Dad..." Zeke prodded his father to release her, for his dad had a bit of a reputation with the ladies, and one that was not always good for business.

"Oh, she knows I'm harmless, now leave me be before I rap you with my cane!" The old man retorted.

"Dad, you don't use a cane."

"Well I'm about to start!"

"Please, could I get a bag of food for Bozeman?" Jessa intervened.

"Zeke!" Ignacious yelled out loud.

"Geez, dad, I'm right here standing next to ya, you don't have to yell my ear off!"

"Oh, there ya are. Ezekiel, this fine little lady needs a fifty-pound bag of your finest high quality dog food for her superior registered animal. I believe this handsome young feller will be obliged to lug it out for her?"

And Ignacious gave Ian a wink.

Zeke sighed. "Alright Ian, I'll show you where. Dad, you behave yourself!" And with that the two younger men left to load the food.

Watching until the door closed behind them, Ignacious once again took hold of Jessa to implore her to not give up hope.

"He will be back, 'Pumpkin'. I didn't get to be this old and crotchety without knowing a thing or two about people. He is so smart it doesn't matter what that television says, Mr. Franklin will pull through!"

Jessa was amazed at how much relief she could eek out of this old man's words. "Thank you Ignacious, I needed to hear that! It is exactly what I have been telling Bozeman, but everyone besides you and I think otherwise." And as Jessa leaned forward and kissed the old man's forehead the door flew open.

"How does he _do_ that?" Zeke demanded incredulously.

Ignacious' hands flew up wildly. "I was just tellin' Missus Franklin about the time that cougar cub got lost and came here lookin' for food and spilled some fish outta the tank and messed up the jerky bin! Why, the newspaper headline read "Riley's Trading Post Ravaged By Vicious Mountain Cat!" They always did make a mountain out of a mole hill, and that's what they did with your man's story, you'll see."

"I am certain you are right, Mr. Riley." Jessa smiled warmly at Ignacious, whose gray sweatshirt swelled with satisfaction at having helped her.

"Zeke?" She inquired. "Are there any available pilots in the area? I would like a flight for three to Montana as soon as possible."

"Ah, no ma'am. You see I was just telling Ian that dad and I were listenin' to the radio, pilot's band that is, when you came up. All non-emergency flights have been canceled until further notice. Seems there is a bad storm that's come up from out of nowhere and they cannot figure out what course it's gonna take. I am sorry, maybe tomorrow you could get one, or the next day."

Jessa stood staring at Zeke for a moment, then paid him and walked out. She let Bozeman into the back of the Suburban then climbed behind the wheel. Her dark hair was speckled with snowflakes like Baby's Breath from a bridal bouquet.

Silently Ian sat across from her as she started the engine and backed away from Riley's post. He wondered aloud what they should do next.

"The bank. They will be tracking any expenses that Grant's credit cards are accumulating, where, when, and what he bought."

"Good idea." Ian agreed, and away they went sloshing through the thickening slush on the roadway. Ten minutes brought them to their destination. Bozeman stayed behind this time while Jessa and Ian stomped their boots before entering the financial institution. There were two tellers, a manager and one other customer. Greetings and an inquiry were made.

"I would like to check the activities of this account please." Jessa handed over her bankcard.

"Oh!" Was all the teller would say before the manager was called over to recheck her findings.

"Oh my. Yes, this is accurate. Mm-hmm, yes. Mrs. Franklin, we have been hoping you would drop by, or if possible both you and your husband. You see here, and again here?" And the manager pointed to two places of particular interest, to him at least, where Grant had made rather large deposits of money. The deposits were two weeks apart, and each for six-digit amounts.

Jessa was more interested in viewing expenditures and so it took a few moments for the impact to reach her, she was incredibly wealthy. "I, I don't understand. What does this mean? Why now? Who signed the checks?"

"Ah, a moment please." And the manager pulled keys

from his pocket as he entered his office. Returning shortly he reviewed with her Grant's record of spending, mostly supplies and parts for equipment and maintenance, travel expenses, and payroll. There were research institutes listed from all over the world that conglomerated to support his team. As more countries joined, the worth of the team increased. "Here we see that Mr. Franklin transferred the payment route from Colorado's geophysicist institute to your, this, address for which we are eternally grateful!" He smiled a big toothy grin. "As for your question "Why now?" I do not know, a change of loyalties perhaps. Having so much money can cause people to rethink whom they can trust. On the bright side it appears Mr. Franklin trusts you implicitly. I am afraid I would not trust my wife to stay with me had I so much money in our joint account." He smirked. "May we interest you in financial counseling, Mrs. Franklin? There are many forms of interest compounding plans available, cd.'s, stock options, etcetera? Hm?"

"No thank you." And Jessa stood to leave.

"Oh! No need to run off, Mrs. Franklin! Are you and your friend free to do lunch? We could talk more then?"

Again Jessa replied "No thank you." And headed for the door.

As Ian reached to open the door for Jessa the manager's hand pulled it wide for her.

"Please, if you ever need anything you have but to ask!" He begged blatantly as they brushed passed him.

Without another word Jessa and Ian left the bank solemnly and climbed back into the Suburban. Bozeman, who had been standing in the back, 'woofed' and wagged his tail, then lie down on his mat as they pulled away from the bank and onto the road.

Jessa steered the Flyer onto the southbound highway and on toward the border of her two beloved countries. In a mere seven hours they could be crossing over. They would stop for lunch first, and in the mid afternoon Jessa once again found herself being questioned by armed security in regards to her reasons for entering the United States of America. Fortunately for her she knew half the men and women working the booths on both sides and they knew her and Grant. After having her open the back of the Suburban and petting Bozeman while giving the vehicle a look see and questioning Ian before checking his passport, the lead officer, whose name Jessa knew was Ben, tipped his hat to her with a smile and motioned for her to proceed.

Not so lucky was the car next to them. Loaded with teenagers, a wisp of suspicious smoke and alcohol, they had been ordered to pull over to the side to have their vehicle searched, dismantled, and then searched some more. Eventually they would be cleared but then they were given the task of putting their car back together.

The slushy snow had been ever so slowly getting drier and fluffier. It was sticking now and everywhere around them the landscape turned to white.

Jessa slowed ever so slightly to compensate for the occasional sticking feeling in the maneuverability of the Flyer. She slowed some more, and then pulled the lever for the four-wheel drive to engage. It gave her better handling as far as turning, yet she knew it would not help her stop on this slick road so she kept her speed to a minimum. The hours seemed to drag on when Ian gently spoke. "Jessa I would like to drive now if it is okay with you. I have had a couple of short naps from want of something better to do, but since I can't quite stretch out, sleeping is out of the question. You see I am at that age where I stiffen easily if I fall asleep in a scrunched position. Take pity on me?" He pleaded.

"Oh, alright. I'm sorry it didn't occur to me. Tunnel vision, you know?"

"Yeah, I think I have that one figured out." He quipped.

Jessa pulled over and they got out to stretch their legs, Bozeman included, then Ian climbed in behind the wheel and Jessa lay on the seat behind him.

The dark day waned into night and yet there were no stars, for the falling snow blocked every kind of light. It came down thickly and had piled high along the sides of the road. Ian had long since slowed the pace even more and few other drivers were taking the risk of being out in it. They were in Montana, this was true, but it may as well have been the surface of the moon for the look of the whiteness in the night. He decided to pull over at the next town and find a motel; perhaps things would look better in the morning.

They were late at finding a room, for hundreds of travelers before them had decided to find a safe haven and let this early winter blizzard run its course. At nearly midnight Ian found a shanty with a sign that still read "VACANCY". He could see why. It was not more than a shack that needed paint, who else would have it? "But at least I'll be able to stretch out." Ian thought wearily. And so with key in hand he returned to the Flyer to wake Jessa. "I have a room for us."

"Oh, you take it. I'm fine in here with Bozeman, if you could bring me a blanket? I don't need more room the way you do. No really, I am not just talking brave, Bozeman does that for me." She smiled. "In the morning I will come in for a shower."

"Well, it's number four over there." And he pointed to a door nearby.

"So scream and I'll come running, alright?" He left for a minute and returned with a warm blanket for her.

Jessa thanked him and offered up a "Goodnight Ian, and thank you for everything. You are an amazing example of Christian friendship."

"I'll try to be content with that. This switch locks all the doors, right?" And pushing it, Ian could hear the locks go down. He also looked at each one to be sure. As for the back doors, they had something better than a lock, a big protective dog.

CHAPTER THIRTEEN

"WE ARE LOOKING FOR JESSICA FRANKLIN"

The chickens were snoozing comfortably as the last bit of light had faded from the cracks and knotholes of their coop. They had barely been active throughout the day for they could not escape the coop to go outside as the door had been locked and besides, it was snowing mightily.

One old hen was so sound asleep her head lay heavily on her wing feathers that now, tucked inside her nest, covered three new eggs for no one had come to collect them.

Suddenly the dust and feathers around her swirled and splattered onto her and her fellow hens. "Whirrwhirrwhirrwhirr" The shocking noise sent the chicken coop full of hens to vibrating violently until the enormous black helicopter's rotating blades screamed to a halt. The two men inside emerged and looked around quickly before racing to the cabin. Knocking briskly more as a protocol than as for politeness, the bigger of the two flung open the wooden door and peered around before calling out with his booming voice, "Mrs. Franklin! Are you here?" And he entered to search Jessa's home, causing her note to fly off the piano and land at his feet. Scooping it up to read quickly the soldier dropped the paper to search the tiny cabin.

The slightly built man stayed outside, watching for any movement from the barn or outbuildings. He saw no humans there or in the surrounding brush or hillsides, but heard frantically cackling chickens. "Westfield!" He called into the cabin. "Find anyone?"

"Naw! She's not here. Better head to the barn, she may be afraid and hiding in there!" And the two raced across the open area to the barn, their eyes darting all the while this way and that for they did not know if they had been seen during their landing.

Entering the barn now the one called Westfield searched through bales of hay and around equipment until his partner announced, "The horses are gone!" It was then he realized "No! Oh no. Would you <u>look</u> at that!"

"Better check to see if it's still in place and functioning." Said Dick as he squatted behind the quad to extract the tracking device. "It's still 'go'. She just didn't take it, rode the animals instead, they're not here."

"Why would she do that?" Westfield shook the bike to hear the slosh of gasoline inside. "It has fuel." He flipped a switch and pushed a button while holding the gas lever. "Vroom!" The bike roared to life. "And it starts right up. Why on this God's green earth didn't she take the motorcycle?" He demanded to know. "Why would she take the time and effort to take those slow poke animals? Doesn't she care about her husband?"

"Actually Doug, it may be that she cares about her animals too. After all, they are here for her when her husband is not. It may mean that she intends to be away a long time to do everything she can for Mr. Franklin, <u>and</u> it's very possible she has not heard as yet, if no one else has come to inform her." Dick looked up at his commander.

Douglas Westfield stared at his partner. "Man, don't you ever get tired of thinking so much?"

Smirking sheepishly Dick replied "That is what they pay me for, remember? Come on, we can be at that lodge in two minutes', airtime. We might even beat her there."

And so the two men ran back to the chopper and in seconds were airborne. Dick was right and with time to spare they again powered down, not to land on the helicopter pad at the end of the airstrip but between the wooden fence and the lodge; the gravel parking lot.

Because of the heavy snowfall the ranch hands had come in early and had a chance to socialize with other guests this evening. All were in good spirits although Mr. And Mrs. Fuller and their family noted Ian's absence in their hearts. Karen had come to play for them and some of the hands found temporary partners to dance with, even Irene had been coaxed by Frank to "cut a rug" as he put it. It was as he twirled her he first noticed a pounding at the windows. The others heard it too. Karen stopped playing and looked up at the people, they were not moving closer to the glass to get a better look at the mystery, but rather to the side in case the rippling glass might shatter. Then a metallic screaming and all was quiet. The people moved quickly now to the windows that at last had stopped their quivering, and peered out. Through the dimly lit darkness of the night ran two figures toward the lodge entrance.

The double doors swung open as the foyer filled with people, Josef and Frank at the lead closely followed by Evelyn and a half dozen burly cowboys. The strangers wore black clothing; wool pants, ribbed turtleneck sweaters, boots and watches, all black but for the snow that stuck to the cloth.

The two parties sized each other up and Westfield, who fairly towered over the rest, spoke first. "Good evening everyone! My friend and I are federal agents of the United States of America." He and Dick showed their id. cards to the crowd. "We are looking for Jessica Franklin, is she here?"

Evelyn came up and held onto Josef's arm as he told Westfield that Mrs. Franklin and their son had left together "This very morning." And assumedly would fly to Montana and that they would probably call tomorrow.

"Sir?" Evelyn asked, "Does this have something to do with Mr. Franklin?"

Westfield darted a glance to Dick before answering her. "It most certainly does ma'am, good evening." And together the two strangers turned to run back to the helicopter. In seconds they were aloft and engulfed by the blizzard.

"Daddy, did that just happen?" Lorene asked, unsure, and Josef nodded to his daughter.

Gram felt numb. "I ain't ever seen anything like it." She softly voiced the feeling of all around her, and the guests began to depart for their cabins, for a very different mood had enveloped them.

The ranch hands however, were fidgety. Frank voiced the feeling everyone seemed to be wrestling with. "You don't think our boy Ian would be in a mess of trouble do you Josef?"

"None that was caused by him Frank, surely not. But I don't know about his friends, maybe? That Grant always was an idea man, maybe somebody else convinced him to use his brains for something he has no business messing with. His wife is so devoted to him, and Ian, well he's maybe got a crush on her."

"I think you hit the nail on the head there boss, I seen it too."

Evelyn broke into their thoughts with "I thought they would say they were here to confirm Grant's death, like when a soldier is killed." She puzzled and Gram agreed, having lost an uncle to war when she was a child.

"No, they didn't want to say much, but I grant you they could. That makes me think they might be back some day." Josef mused, then he and his wife and foreman retired to the lounge to listen to the nightly news.

Above the clouds Westfield ordered "Dick! Power up our nearest satellite, focusing vibrator beams directly south, full power! We have got to catch up with her A.S.A.P.!"

"Aye, sir!"

CHAPTER FOURTEEN

SNOWFALL

Ian awoke with a start and stared into the dark and unfamiliar room. For a moment he believed he was in the den at home, but he was colder here. Realizing it was his own shivering that had awakened him he jumped out of bed with a sheet wrapped around himself, for there had been no other blanket than the one he had given to Jessa, and flipped on the light switch. Nothing happened, the electricity was out. Searching in the dark for his clothes Ian dressed and opened the door. There were no streetlights. He took a few steps to the end of the awning and stretched out an arm, and felt falling snow. One more step and his boot shoved into a snow bank. Upon bending over and setting his hand down he felt more snow. It was two feet deep and still coming down. Carefully Ian stepped into it and made his way to the Suburban's front door to knock gently.

Moments later Jessa's raised hand was groping for the lock to pull it up. Ian opened the door a bit, then had to scoop snow away with his hands to open it completely. Kicking snow from his boots as he stepped in and closed the door he found the keys and started the engine, then went out again to dig away from the exhaust pipe so that fumes would not back up into the vehicle.

Upon his return a sleepy Jessa asked him "The sun isn't up yet, is there something wrong?"

"Well, by the time we will be able to go anywhere it will be high above us, I'm afraid. The power is out all around us because of the snow, and until we see a plow going by we are stuck!"

"How much is there?" Jessa asked incredulously as she sat upright. Pulling a flashlight out from under the front seat and shining it through a window she saw a brilliantly sparkling white landscape made up of billions and billions of tiny thick puffs of frozen water landing ever so lightly, one upon another.

"I'll go back to the room for my stuff, then go on walk about to see if there are lights elsewhere. Shall I take Bozeman with me to make yellow snow?"

"Woof!" Bozeman agreed from the back, standing now with ears up and tail beating the back of the seat and the rear doors.

Smiling at last Jessa replied to them both "Of course you boys can go out and play in the snow."

Ian opened a back door for Bozeman who leaped out onto the snow, halting only a moment to realize his legs were buried up to his belly and to rethink his mode of movement. Now the great dog leaped and plunged, leaped and plunged, until a staggering Ian coaxed him under the awning that curved around the end of the motel and out of sight.

Jessa picked up her boots and climbed over the back of the front seat to slide onto it and pull them on. She kept the Suburban running, for Ian had filled the tank before coming to the motel for the night. She checked the clock. It read five forty five; an hour before sunrise. It was a good thing the tank was full. "Well Flyer, it seems we are grounded." Jessa spoke wistfully and turned on the radio.

Twenty minutes had gone by before Ian and Bozeman returned, and both were breathing hard from the exertion of trudging and leaping through the deep snow. Ian opened the back doors for the panting dog that was more than ready to stand on something solid that would not give way and swallow him up. He had used up any puppy like antics that were in him and soon lay down.

After first catching his breath, Ian reported. "Okay, about a mile and a half away to the south are the rest of the city's lights, for now anyway. I could see there has been a plow on a nearby street and I think I heard it, so hopefully it will be coming around here soon. If not, we will be getting hunger served for breakfast. Now don't you wish we had stopped for supper last night?" But he was smiling at their adventure.

After the blackness of the night was coaxed away by a dimly lit gray hue, a snowplow came chugging up the hill. Using the flashlight Ian was able to get the driver's attention for him to do a U- turn in the parking lot so that all the would-be travelers would not be long term residents in the crusty old building. The driver came in on the far side of the lot and cleared the perimeter so that the snow piled high in the middle with a free lane all around it. Waving his thanks, Ian returned to the Suburban to dig away the last few feet of snow behind the rear tires.

He puffed to Jessa "I'll take the blanket back to the room, then we can check out and go hunt for breakfast. Do you need to use it?"

"No, I'm fine. Maybe the next place will look more inviting." She hoped aloud as she frowned at the paint-peeled motel. Some of the shutters were hanging loose and tilted and its overall appearance was dirty, even under its freshly whitened roof.

"Alright, I'll be right back." And he disappeared into the room. A moment only had passed when Jessa heard a loud "CRACK!" And the roof took a sudden three-foot drop where Ian had been standing.

Bozeman was barking wildly.

"Ian!" Jessa shrieked as she threw herself from the Flyer to clear as much of the distance as she could, and scrambled on hands and knees to the rippled aluminum awning that had also broken free and fallen to the ground. Startled screams and yelling could be heard throughout the rickety building now, for not one person was left asleep.

"Stay back! I'm, alright!" Ian coughed. "Ouch! I'm coming out!" He shouted as dust and broken bits of glass and sheet rock poured out from under the awning.

Emerging from the rubble he was covered in white gritty

dust, with a trickle of blood oozing from his right temple. But what worried Jessa was the way Ian held his right arm.

"Oh dear God!" She exclaimed quickly before shouting at the top of her lungs "We need help over here!" At the people milling about the intact portion of the building, most of them were for the first time realizing that it had been snowing heavily all night long, for they had retired long before the Flyer had arrived.

Jessa left Ian only long enough to climb back to the open door of the Suburban and snatch her cell phone to call for help, while thanking God for Irene once more as she realized how thorough Evelyn's assistant had been in charging the battery for her.

Returning in moments to Ian and a few brave volunteers, a visiting firefighter returning home from a training, a construction worker on a family vacation, and a businessman taking a sales seminar, Jessa called

9-1-1 to ask for an ambulance.

The firefighter had brought his trauma kit and helped Ian get out of his coat, then handed it to Jessa to hold around Ian's good shoulder for warmth and comfort, and because she needed to be near. Ron, as he had introduced himself, dabbed at Ian's forehead and temple, cleaning the wound with a beta dine solution before bandaging and wrapping it. Then came the displaced shoulder caused by a beam that had hit Ian from above and behind. A few inches closer and it would have killed him, or worse.

Carefully the shirt was removed to expose the injured shoulder. "Aw!" And Ian gritted his teeth in pain, while the firefighter trained as an Emergency Medical Technician, or 'E.M.T.', talked him into looking into the crowd to guess which one of them was a clown.

"What?" Ian squinted at the people.

Jessa knew what the 'E.M.T.' was doing for she had done it herself in times gone by, a million years ago? Back at home with her folks before she married Grant.

"Aah! Geez!" Ian cried aloud as the firefighter, who had

diverted his attention momentarily with his off-the-wall question, had simultaneously lifted and rotated his shoulder to slip it back into its socket.

It hurt like heck, but it worked. A handful of snow was placed upon the swollen shoulder and Ian tested it. "Not bad, thank you!" He tried to smile.

"Do you still think you want a rescue unit? They're pricey and you <u>could</u> drive to an urgent care facility, I have an address for one nearby and you could have an x-ray if it will make you feel better. Ian took his advice, besides, all the while he was being attended to, the firefighter's portable radio had been squawking with other calls for help, and all of them were snow related. There were those who had not pulled over to wait out the storm, they had slid off the road and hit telephone poles, or each other. Some had been reported missing in a snow bank. One destroyed electrical pole had lit up the night sky and caused the outage. The power company was working on it, so the 'E.M.T.' used his radio to tell dispatch to cancel this one rescue call to the motel.

The owner approached them. "Mr. Fuller, I don't know what to say, please forgive me for not tearing down this old building sooner. I had plans to get started remodeling next spring, but I guess that money can go to any lawsuit you might be thinking of. The man handed Ian a bulging envelope. "Here are the night's earnings. It may be enough to cover an x-ray and some pain pills, and a much better motel stay than I can offer you. I sure am sorry, but I <u>am</u> grateful you weren't killed, sir." And tears welled up in the man's eyes as he looked up at his caved in roof.

Sympathy surged in Ian's heart for this struggling businessman. He knew for himself what it was like to try to attract customers to a private company, or to be thinking up new entertainments and activities for them.

"First of all," Ian began "I forgive you, it was not your fault. And I am all right, or will be soon enough. Thank you for your sympathy and concern. I have never sued anyone and certainly won't for something that you had no control over. There was not sufficient warning about this storm nor the amount of precipitation. If this were two feet of water we might be in worse shape. Look, it was the right gesture and I appreciate it, but you need this more than I do." And Ian handed the envelope of cash back to the distraught owner of the motel, who could not hold back his emotions any longer and excused himself to cry in private, for never had such an incredible act of kindness been done for him, and when he fully expected to lose his business, his livelihood, to the weather.

After the construction worker helped him to stand up, Ian thanked everyone for coming to his rescue, and then the man helped him through the snow and into the Suburban. Ian scooted across to the co pilot's seat rather than try to walk around. Jessa climbed in behind the wheel after thanking everyone, then helped Ian with his seat belt. The Flyer's engine was already warm since it had been running all this time and with the doors now shut it warmed quickly inside, much to the relief of a shivering Ian. He watched as the others loaded their vehicles to leave.

Jessa drove to the edge of the darkness and into lit city streets. "You did a good thing back there, and I'm proud of you." She told him as she stared straight ahead. "You know, for a moment I thought I had lost you. I didn't like the thought of that." She choked and started to cry.

"You'd better pull over, there's a spot." He pointed and realized his own eyes were misting over as well.

The engine was shut off and the parking break set. Ian's seatbelt 'clicked' loose and he slid over to hold her in his arms, disregarding any pain for the opportunity to be closer to her. The minutes passed with quiet weeping until Ian could stand it no longer and made to kiss her lips. She quickly turned her face to offer him her cheek, which he accepted gratefully and lingered there. She returned the favor but with a peck only, for it was all she could allow and wept for her own ineptness at being able to show him what he meant to her.

"It's alright," he told her gently "it's enough. I know that you love me. Thank you for letting it show a little." And Ian wept for joy.

Jessa gathered herself enough to pull back onto the highway and search for the address of the urgent care facility for a check- up by a sincere young intern, before searching for a nice hotel where they could clean up, as Ian was still covered in dust and they had not eaten since midday yesterday.

Jessa chose the cleanest, biggest and most expensive hotel around, but cost did not matter anymore for she was rich and Ian was worth any price.

CHAPTER FIFTEEN

BOZEMAN, MONTANA

Jessa could not help herself. She could not stop smiling as she listened for one more second to the happy song Ian was singing as he showered. It was nonsense and silliness, a love struck tune he made up as he went along. She closed and locked the door of the suite behind her and went swinging down the immaculate hallway of the fifth floor to take the elevator to the lobby, where she had noticed a manikin in the window that wore a dress similar to the one Lorene had loaned her. She remembered Ian's open mouth as she had come down the stairs, a mere two days ago? The still, small voice inside her was asking "Are you sure you want to do this? Is it fair?" She told the voice to be quiet, that Ian deserved the best in a breakfast companion and she was going to be it. Through the lobby window she could be seen with an attendant of the shop. Jessa pointed to the velvety red, double strapped slip of a dress and went to the changing room to try it on. It fit much better than Lorene's had and the hotel was warm, not at all like the den at the lodge. She bought it on her card along with black-strapped Stiletto heels and inquired about a styling salon, which the attendant took her to. There she was pampered, washed and coiffed. There were no other customers and in a crisp half hour the backwoods waif was once again transformed into a glamorous starlet.

From the salon she made the call he had been waiting restlessly for, and bypassing the slow elevators to fly down the stairs a dapper, tuxedo- clad Ian met Jessa at the salon in under two minutes and together, arm in arm they strolled through the lobby and through a corridor to the hotel's five star restaurant for a tantalizing interlude with fantasy.

They allowed themselves a time just for them. There were no problems or fears of foreboding. They talked and laughed, ate and drank as if they had always been free to do so, and when it was time to face reality again they were able to meet it with an understanding of what life could be like if they were together always, and they kept that tucked away in their hearts for the days ahead. There was no sexual innuendo or promise of its purchase, for they were not free to dream that dream, yet. Then it was time to continue their journey, for reality will always have its way. As they were about to leave the restaurant they stopped, knowing the real world awaited them just beyond, and Ian bent low to Jessa's upturned cheek for one last lingering kiss, then out they strode together to the elevators to continue their journey.

Bozeman had spent the last three hours in the parking lot in the back of the Suburban with food and water, and now he pricked up his ears and barked, thus startling a little girl who had emerged from her family's car.

After allowing the great dog a few minutes with the trees and bushes it was into the Flyer and on down the highway. Jessa wore her jeans and boots again to put pedal to metal for finally it had stopped snowing and within the next few miles there was little sign of it at all.

Ian read the road sign out loud "Bozeman, Montana, two hundred seventy five miles. Aren't you going to call your folks yet?" He thought it odd that Jessa had made no attempt to contact them.

"Heh- heh." She laughed quietly to herself as much as in answer to his question. "My parents are technologically challenged, and since their children have moved out their answering machine does not get used. They do not think to check it when it is on and that is only when I, or one of my siblings show up for a visit and reset it for them. And also, if I call ahead mom will knock herself out cleaning the house until she is exhausted, drive to the pet shop to buy another fish to pass off as Freddy, whom I had as a pet in high school but since I left I have counted five different fish that she has presented as Freddy, and she will buy out the grocery store to feed me every two hours as if I were still a baby." Jessa grimaced.

"Wow, that's rough!" And Ian rolled his eyes.

"Hey, is there no sympathy?" Jessa joked with him.

"None whatsoever. Your parents have raised up a highly intelligent, loyal, strong and beautiful woman. You have no sympathy because you don't need it and I know that whatever happens, Jessa will come out on top."

At hearing such high praise she could only glance at him and blush gratefully. How long had it been since Grant had thought to praise her? Of late his words had pertained to the work he was involved in and not much else, leaving her feeling pangs of loneliness even when they were together.

CHAPTER SIXTEEN

ALIVE!

"Miss Cho, Miss Cho!" A soldier approached her on the rain soaked hillside; others were following him with pickaxes and shovels, anything that could be used for excavating bodies from the mud.

The rain had fallen for fifty-one days and at times torrentially, though now it was hardly more than a mere spray, and yet it would not stop.

The soldier grabbed her shovel and pried her blistered hands from it, then moved in closer to whisper, "Mai- Ling, you must stop now and rest.

If your own exhaustion should cause you to speak unwisely, then your father's plan for your freedom will be in vain." Then adding so others nearby could hear, "Miss Cho, there are more rescue workers now and you have been here too long already. Go to the tent the Americans have erected, there." And he pointed to the foot of the hill they stood on. "They have hot tea and rice. You must eat and drink now. If you like I will walk you there myself." His concern for her welled up in his eyes, he would miss his cousin dearly.

Her own almond shaped eyes, so full of despair, met his own. She was simply too exhausted to argue anymore, and relented. Her lifetime of obedience was at work for her in this and she bowed her head to him and turned to trudge and slide down the mountainside, over clumps of mud and around boulders, uprooted trees and rubbish, under a constant pelting of rain. Her boots were soaked inside, her hands numb from constant hours of digging, searching for her father who had been an interpreter for the international team of global seismologists, Chinese being one of the few languages they as yet had to contract out, and Mai Ling's father had had hopes of being allowed a permit to travel with them worldwide, and bring his daughter.

At last she slid onto the main road to follow it to the large tarpaulin tent set up by the international Red Cross unit assigned to this sector of the mountain. Thousands of workers were digging and hauling away debris, coming and going everywhere in the muck which was her home. Some were soldiers, others were villagers looking for family, and some were imports from other countries here to help. They would have come sooner had her government allowed them in, but hers was a proud people and not given to showing their need. She saw now what it took to make them bend.

Mai- Ling was about to lift open the tent flap when she heard a sound, a person perhaps? She stopped to listen and looked at one of the storage shacks...

"Oooh, God help me!"

In that moment it could not have been clearer who it was and Mai- Ling ran to where the voice emanated. Behind barrels and boxes of provisions lay a rain soaked, mud splattered scientist she had known through her father allowing her to attend them on the mountain, and she cried tears of joy. "Mista Frankwin! You live! Let me help you, I will get help, I..."

At once Grant's hands took hold of her arms as she rose to get help. "No!" His cracking voice whispered frantically. "Mai-Ling you must not tell anyone! They must not know! Promise me, please!"

She was hesitant but complied. "But who must not know?"

"Your government, and mine." He begged with tear-streaked face and Mai- Ling could not refuse him, this man befriended and confided in by her father.

She gushed the news of the tragedy to him and they cried

together over their losses, and then hatched a plan to get them both out of the country. Mai-Ling brought hot tea and rice enough for them both, then procured bandages and wrapped his bruised and cracked ribs before helping Grant into his yellow jump suit once more and onto his feet.

She told him to stay put for a while longer and returned in a jeep being driven by her cousin, and together the three of them rode to the far side of the mountain, passing more tarpaulin tents and rivers choked with houses, trees and rubbish. As they climbed the winding, now muddied road to the hospital above, had they looked back they could have seen the last tent going up. Embossed across it read "Adventist Development and Relief Agency".

CHAPTER SEVENTEEN

ADVENTIST FIRE

"Welcome to Bozeman, Montana!" Ian read aloud from the driver's seat, rousing Jessa from her R.E.M. state. Ever since leaving the ranch and doing something positive in search of Grant she had been able to enjoy sleeping again. There were no more nightmares forcing screaming fits from her lips to frighten her dog or anyone else that might be nearby. She sat up and stretched luxuriously, then picking up her boots she slid over and down onto the passenger side at the window. 'Clicking' on her seatbelt and reaching into the glove compartment she pulled out a hairbrush and set to grooming her tousled tresses.

Ian glanced over and smiled. "Looking forward to seeing your folks?" He queried.

"Always. It's been too long, and I never know what they will be up to next. Since they retired they bought a motor home and go- go- go! They have taken to exploring their world, and I am so glad they have that chance to enjoy life. Take a left here and then a right at the second light."

Leaving the mainstream of traffic and downtown, the Flyer pulled onto a long graveled driveway. There was a modest two-story home with an outbuilding that had in days gone by been used for a kennel, and a cyclone fence going all around the backyard and the kennel. There were no dogs in it these days, but something always pointed to the hobby of the day. After ringing the doorbell of the house to no avail Jessa, Ian and Bozeman walked to the fence. No one was there, but there was a new sound. Upon entering and conducting an investigation they discovered four rock tumblers in motion, two rock saws, and tubs and barrels filled with rocks. There were also bowls of polished rocks and windows covered with cut rocks that had been placed and glued into flowered formations, the colors and patterns were surprisingly beautiful for something off of the ground. Jessa smiled at the productivity of her parents as she headed for the gate, then kneeling down to Bozeman and hugging her dog while stating, "stay" she closed and latched the gate and left with Ian to look for her parents.

The motor home was parked under the awning, but the minivan her parents drove was gone from the garage. After consulting her watch Jessa announced "They may be out shopping or having a late lunch, dad likes a slice of pizza now and then." She went to the driver's side door and climbed in, started the engine but then shut it off, for a pickup truck with the local fire department emblem on its side had pulled up behind them. Smiling, Jessa slid off the seat and strode to greet Frank, a long time friend of hers, her family, and of Grant. After a burly bear hug and introductions, and Frank had riding with him a young man in training, he bellowed at the freckle faced, red haired, skinny trainee, "Skip, radio the station to set some vittles on for a former member and her friend!"

"Yes, sir!" The probationary member, or 'probie', responded enthusiastically, eager to please his chief.

"Belay that order please!" Jessa retorted while folding her arms. "Frank, you are doing it again, making plans for me without asking. I would love to visit the station again but another time will have to do. There are things that need to be cleared up first." And she declined to say more on the matter. "But maybe you can help me find mom and dad?" She asked hopefully.

"Kitten, don't you know what day this is?" The chief asked of her incredulously.

"Saturday I think, what, isn't it?"

At her befuddled answer Frank laughed. "Heh heh. Jessica, your parents have been bitten by the Adventist bug that has been swarming throughout this neighborhood. Your in laws and your, ahem, ex boyfriend have gotten this town on its knees, so to speak."

Stunned, Jessa felt a warm glow rising up from within. "That's wonderful." She realized mistily. "It's a dream come true, and now I know where to find them! Thank you Frank!" And smiling brightly Jessa ran to the Flyer and restarted the engine, fortunately waiting for them to exit the drive and thus giving Ian a chance to catch up. Frank pulled aside and watched as the Flyer backtracked itself into the downtown area.

"Now there goes a good daughter, Skip." Frank said to his trainee. "She has been trying to get her folks to join her, her husband and his folks in going to church and getting religion, now it has happened. This is a happy day, let's eat!" As he steered out into the road, in his rear view mirror Frank glanced back to see Bozeman at the gate, ears up and staring up the road at a cable service truck and the two men working the line, or appearing to. Something about the two did not seem right, but he could not put his finger on it and made a mental note to do a drive by, but after lunch.

Breezing on into the downtown area again Jessa crossed the highway and headed toward a large parking lot filled with cars that surrounded a beautiful, orange brick building that was A-framed at the top and sported a large white steeple that shone from within.

"There's their van!" She pointed excitedly to a white minivan with small red striping on both sides. The Flyer sidled alongside and parked.

"Are we dressed alright?" Ian wanted to know.

And looking him up and down with a grin Jessa replied, "Better in our jeans than a skimpy dress and tuxedo, I'm thinking. We seem to have trouble with in between, don't we?"

And they marched through the double door entrance.

Once inside they were greeted with smiles and handshakes and given a program of activities, classes, and doctrinal beliefs, and since it was late in the morning Sabbath school classes were over and the people had moved into the main sanctuary for announcements, music, prayer and a sermon.

Through the overhead speakers in the foyer could be heard the sermon emanating from within the sanctuary, and as Jessa and Ian walked toward the huge room of pews filled with worshipers, she found herself focusing on the voice more than the words it spoke. "David?" She whispered quizzically.

Upon entering the large and beautiful room they were hard pressed to find a pew that had room for two, but a deacon was quick to help them and they settled in.

Ian admired the craftsmanship of the three angels adorning the wall behind the pastor. They were of carved wood and painted a golden hue; each held a trumpet and an open scroll. "The three angels of Revelation fourteen, I presume?" He had guessed accurately, and that each had a message to proclaim.

The spectacled, wiry young pastor with slicked back short brown hair had paused for a moment as he sometimes did for emphasis, no one need know it was because his breath caught inside him when these latest visitors had entered. The man he did not know, but the woman he knew very well. A moment, and he continued.

"Beloved, time is soon to come to an end, yet do not fear for it is the beginning of eternity with Jesus for those who will believe! The bible tells us that there will be wars and rumors of wars. There will be earthquakes in many places. Men will run to and fro, and knowledge will increase. Justice will be confused, and even love will fall into an unnatural state where men will marry men, children will hate their parents, and parents will do the un- thinkable to their children.

I ask you is this not the world we live in today? The Middle East is constantly at war! And now they have found a way to drag us into the fray, our own great nation has been attacked by terrorists numerous times. Tens of thousands have died in various earthquakes in the last six months alone! Look at the technological advancements in the last fifty years, few ideas of which existed a century ago! What do we hear on the news every day? Every day murder has been committed, rape, robbery, kidnapping. Abuses unspeakable that were <u>never</u> meant to be! These are the results of sin, for the wages of sin is death! If there were no sin there would be no death, no disease such as Aids, no diseased liver from alcohol, no lung cancer from smoking, no heart disease from overeating, sloth or stress.

My friends <u>we</u> have Jesus to look up to as our example! Those who do not know Him have not His example. How can we show others that we have but to live His example to be happy? We must study the bible daily and keep the commandments given us! These are not arbitrary rules set upon us by a dictatorial leader, not at all! These are guidelines given us with love and compassion by a loving compassionate God, who knows the trials we will face throughout our lives, and by following these guidelines we honor Him, and ourselves as well!

All are invited to adjourn to our fellowship meal as soon as we recite them once again, for only if we keep them in our hearts will we not stumble and fall prey to the enemy."

And pastor Dave began with "And in Exodus twenty God speaks all these words. 'You shall have no other gods before me, You shall not worship any idol, You shall not misuse the name of God, <u>Remember</u> the Sabbath day to keep it holy', now church I want you to take notice that these first four commandments create a bond between us the worshiper and God our creator. The next six show us how to live harmoniously with each other. 'Honor your father and your mother, you shall not murder, you shall not commit adultery', now I <u>must</u> clarify what adultery is. Having sexual intercourse without being married to that person is adultery plain and simple and there is no getting around it. The world is teaching that as long as you are eighteen years old and not using someone else's spouse, then if it feels good do it and you will be okay. That is a false teaching! <u>Only</u> within the sanctity of marriage is this special intimacy ordained by God! I see you sitting there squirming in your seats so I know I have made my point!" And without humor Dave paused for emphasis before continuing. " 'You shall not steal, you shall not lie, you shall not covet your neighbor's house, spouse, or servant, or anything that is your neighbor's!' Now folks, we already know that our neighbor is anyone we meet, anywhere. Not only Dick and Jane and their kids living over the fence from us, but also the people we meet on the street, or that live under it. Our neighbors are all around us when we drive, cutting us off in traffic or speeding on by to make it under the light while we are left behind. These are our neighbors. They also live in far away lands with different skin colors and cultures than we have, different religions even. Yes, they are all our neighbors that our God commands us to respect!

Now I ask you, Can we be happy if we forever want more and more things? Particularly in this country I should think, there is more stuff to covet than there has ever been in the history of the world! We are being tempted at every angle to want more stuff, a new car, a second car, and a bigger and fancier home. Commercials bombard our big screen televisions with new and improved stuff. Is it possible to log onto the Internet without advertisements for more stuff? If there is then please let me know!" He smiled. "Signs and billboards selling more stuff fill our sight as we drive, radio stations stay on the air by selling us stuff. Our friends and coworkers want to show us their <u>new</u> stuff, especially if it is stuff that no one else has yet! Oh yes that is the very <u>best</u> kind of stuff to have, and they feel fulfilled by that! For a day, or a week. Until you and I and others can get the same stuff or the upgraded stuff! Friends, Jesus was, is and always will be the **<u>BEST</u>** thing that can happen in your life!

"Amen! Praise God! Hallelujah!" Excited members of the congregation agreed.

"Please do not let the worldly pursuit of stuff, which is coveting, come between you and your pursuit of the everlasting kingdom of God!"

Smiling now pastor Dave continued, 'A time of trouble shall fall upon the land, unlike the world has ever known'. No amount of stuff can save you and me, or our families. But only by the blood of Christ who died on the cross to buy us back from the maker and manipulator of sins, can we be saved from our sins, and <u>all</u> have sinned and come short of the glory of God!"

Do you want to leave this tired old world and live forever without the pain and suffering we see every day?

"Yes! Amen! Come Lord Jesus!" Came fervent shouts from the flock.

"Then let us pray." And all bowed their heads. "Dear Father in heaven, we thank you for our lives today. We thank you that we have this beautiful sanctuary in which to come together and worship you our creator, and can learn more about your plan for us through your word to us, the holy bible. Thank you Abba, that we enjoy our religious freedom without fear of death or jail, or ridicule, for yet a little while longer. Help us to share examples of your love to those we meet on the street, in our work, in our daily lives so that all may make their decision to follow you and then the end may come, and a new beginning may bring us to heaven to live and worship at thy feet forevermore. In Jesus' precious and holy name we do pray, amen."

And every voice spoke it, "Amen."

"And please remember that the word gospel means good news!

So start your day with a little <u>good news</u> every day and see what a difference it, and <u>you</u>, can make!" Dave smiled at his flock.

At that the pastor walked down the center aisle as he normally did while the deacons excused the people pew by pew. He would stand in the foyer and shake the hand of every person if they were so inclined, but today he stopped near the back and leaned over to take the hand of a pretty young woman and asked if he could escort her to the fellowship hall for a delicious vegetarian buffet. Jessa hugged him and together they strode out of the sanctuary, through the foyer, down a long hall between classrooms and into the fellowship hall.

Inside the huge room were thirty round tables having white linen cloths with flower arrangements on them, cushioned metal chairs all around the tables and several oblong tables laden with vegetarian food of all sorts from hot and steamy entrees to cold tossed salads and desserts. There was a table for bread and condiments, and one for juice, tableware and napkins. David and Jessa had been so intense in greeting each other that Ian fell behind in the crowd and had not been introduced until now. As people poured in through more double doors and milled around at tables to wait for friends and family or to line up near the food, pastor Dave asked for them to bow their heads once more as he asked for the Lord's blessing upon the food, and the hands that had prepared it, and for it to strengthen and nourish their bodies. Visitors and parents with small children were invited to partake first, and then the rest of the congregation joined in. Dave always waited to the end to serve himself and Jessa would not leave him for she wanted to know everything that had happened to him since she had called it off between them, especially the part about how he went from street kid to a business suit wearing pastor of a large congregation.

He cleared his throat at that, and mockingly straightened his tie before announcing, "I think that was what it took. I had to lose the person I cared about the most before I could look at things seriously. And I remembered a lot of what you had been telling me, and started to search the scriptures. You know me Jess; I have to learn it for myself. I could have saved myself a lot of agony had I been able to accept on faith what others have learned. And here comes my wife." He motioned with outstretched arm.

From the kitchen approached a slender young woman with shortly cropped brown hair having a smooth, gliding elegance in her walk. She was a vision of self-assurance, capable and discerning. She was perfectly suitable pastor's wife material. She removed her apron and placed it over a chair before approaching them, then greeted her husband with a peck on his cheek before taking his hand. "Ellen, this is the other woman you have heard so much about." Dave informed his wife.

Ellen cocked her head sideways at Jessa for a moment as she often did when meeting someone for the first time. Jessa began to feel uncomfortable. Was Ellen the jealous type? She almost flinched when Ellen made a sudden move toward her but then she was suddenly glad she had not, for the woman threw her arms around her shoulders in gushing gratitude.

"I have thanked God for you often, Jessa! If it had not been for your strength our David would be in jail, or worse! Through you our Lord has worked to change his heart, and now through David our Lord is working on everyone in this room to come to Him! Take a look around you at the many stars in your crown, everyone is here because you and others like you have stood for righteousness, have spoken up for God rather than ducking your head into the sand when adversity comes, or a simple chance to share our faith. If you had chosen David over God, well, I would not be here, and about half of the people in this room, including that couple near the wall! I believe you know them?" And Ellen gave Jessa a winning smile as she pointed above the sea of tables to the farthest wall, where her parents were sitting down to table with their plates.

It was almost too good to be true. "If only Grant were here it would all be perfect." Jessa thought. Now it was her turn to be grateful. "Thank you Ellen! I love you already!" She laughed. "Please excuse me, both of you! Jessa took Ian by the sleeve to steer him through the sea of tables and wandering people.

He was a little disappointed at not being led to the food tables, as they appeared to be dwindling in full dishes, but that would have to wait he sighed, yet he found himself looking forward to meeting her parents.

Wesley and Yvonne James were getting themselves settled, and it probably was a good thing they were sitting down when suddenly their youngest daughter was kneeling between them and kissing their cheeks shamelessly, an arm around each one of them. "I love you mom! I love you dad!"

Dad spluttered "What the? Oh it's you Jessica!" And he laughed. "I thought it was my birthday or something to have such a nice present!"

Mom was holding onto her daughter and whispering in her ear, my baby, my baby." And her eyes glistened with liquid joy.

Jessa also cried for her happiness at seeing her parents integrated in the faith. "I'm so happy you both are here and we will be in the kingdom with our Lord! I have prayed for you over the years that somehow the Holy Spirit would reach you. You have always been good to me and I thank God for you both!"

As mom wiped her eyes with a napkin and replaced her glasses to look at her daughter she reproached her. "Jessa you have gotten so skinny! You *must* go and eat right now! Hurry and get some food before it is all gone!" And to Ian "Yes, yes hello whoever you are, please take Jessica to the food tables first, then we will get to know one another!" And Ian could not have liked Yvonne any more than at that moment.

Now it was his turn to take Jessa by the sleeve and he led her to the buffet. Without asking what it was first he scooped and tossed food upon his plate in heaps until there was no more room, thinking that Bozeman had been eating more regularly than he.

Watching them go, mom handed a pill to dad from her purse, then put one in her mouth as well and sipped some water. There was no need to burden their daughter with their ill health, after all, why spoil their happy reunion? Next she took the cane she had placed upon the empty chair next to her and slid it under the table.

Returning with food-laden plates Jessa introduced Ian as her bodyguard and friend, and her parents commented on hearing about him before from Grant. "So where is Grant these days?" Wesley wanted to know. Of course the question would arise. Taking her time to chew the first bite of her dinner roll and swallow first, Jessa filled them in on the drama of her life.

Mom inhaled quickly. "China! Oh but sweetheart! They jail missionaries over there for preaching the bible!"

Dad added, "And our countries have been close to, well, war. I will say it and apologize for scaring anybody but you know it may very well fulfill prophecy about the time of trouble at the end, 'such as the world has never seen in the history of the world'. You know they want Taiwan back since that little self-proclaimed country has been making it on their own!"

Mom changed the uncomfortable subject. "Did you stop by the house first, dear?" She asked hopefully.

"Yes of course, but why would you ask? We rang the

doorbell several times and checked around back; good job you two! I'm impressed with the artistry!" And dad beamed at her compliment.

"So there was no answer from the house? From your sister I mean?" Mom asked hopefully.

A shocked pause met them. "No, there was no one there, or so I thought. Oh no, is Debra back? Is she on another binge?" Jessa had to know.

"Well you know how lonely she gets when Tom is long hauling. Texas, isn't it dad?" And Yvonne nudged her husband under the table to play along.

"What? Oh, right. Yeah, that could be the place I guess." And dad excused himself to the bathroom.

Ian went back to the buffet for seconds and dessert.

Alone now, the two women looked each other in the eye, and mom looked away. "Alright, I am sorry. I wasn't exactly truthful. He left her and has moved to Texas to be with his family."

"Oh no. I thought this would happen but never wanted it. I thought he would be the one that could snap her out of her depression. If only he would have taken a local job and stayed put, I think they could have made it."

Ian returned to enjoy his food. The first plateful he had scarffed up so hastily he had not experienced to the fullest its merit. "Mmm, this is good, is there peanut butter in this?" He asked Yvonne while holding a forkful in the air for her to see.

"Yes, in fact it is called peanut butter loaf. I can get you the recipe if you would like?"

"Thank you, I appreciate that." Ian smiled at Yvonne and took another appreciative bite. Yvonne offered, "In fact, part of the Adventist Message is good health through vegetarianism and temperance. Also," she ventured carefully, "Wes and I are enjoying better health these days because of following this diet, and getting our exercise and making sure we get our rest and drinking lots of water. He has quit smoking and alcohol and I no longer drink coffee that robs my body of much needed calcium.

And," she added cautiously "we are keeping our diabetes under control through diet."

Jessa's breath caught "Diabetes, mom?"

"Borderline, dear. When Grant's parents heard about it they relentlessly struggled with us until we gave in and adopted a lifestyle change, bless their hearts!"

"Did they visit or leave word that they were going to China with A.D.R.A?" Jessa begged for information.

"Oh no sweetheart, they had gone before anyone in the community knew about it, except the church secretary, that is. Darlene made the arrangements for them."

Pastor Dave and his family approached. He announced to Jessa "I have come to crow proudly! This is Matthew, Timothy and Bethany. Kids, please say hello to Mrs. Franklin." The two boys greeted her in unison but the tow headed little girl would only hide her face in her mother's skirt.

Jessa was thrilled to be included in their lives but also felt segregated, for she had no offspring to introduce to these adorable children. "Wouldn't it be grand?" She thought, "If our children could be friends?" It tugged at her heartstrings just as it had when others had introduced their children to her.

They all chatted for a long while, enjoying everything about the atmosphere of the situation. It was like one big family or school reunion day. It was like when Jesus will come again and all the righteous will be brought into heaven.

Dave stood and raised his arms for everyone's attention. "Folks, there is a need for special prayer here, let us now bow our heads. "Dear Father in heaven, we are your people and do come to you with a heavy burden, one which we cannot bear alone and so ask that you lift it from us. We are missing Grant, Abba. He has been taken from our fold into a far away land and for reasons we know not, he has not returned at the appointed hour. We ask that you comfort and guide him, while uplifting him spiritually. Send your mighty angels to surround him and protect him, and please bring him home to us again oh LORD as you have done so many times already in your safe and loving arms, but not our will Father but thine own be done, here on earth as it is in heaven, for you are our rock and our salvation, in Jesus' name we pray, amen." And the very room reverberated with voices in unison "Amen."

Gratefully Jessa thanked David for leading them out in prayer, she hugged him and Ellen also, then it was time for a little cleanup which she and Ian helped with, for as was a popular saying in their church "Many hands make light work."

Dad approached to tell Jessa that mom had gone to the van with her empty dishes and that they would meet them at home. "Alright, we'll be along shortly too, dad." And she hugged him.

"It has been wonderful seeing you again, Jess." David said as he hugged her one last time. "I wish you and Grant would move back home, there is certainly room in this town for your talents and abilities. I would love to hear you sing for us on any Sabbath, or any time for that matter, though I am sure you don't feel much like it right now. I'm sorry, you are going through a rough time and here I am thinking of myself."

"That's alright David. I truly believe it is going to be alright." She assured him.

David gazed at Jessa a moment longer, admiring her strength, then excused himself to take his family home.

CHAPTER EIGHTEEN

WHAT'S WITH BOZEMAN?

Ian and Jessa climbed into the Flyer and headed for her folk's house. Upon entering the driveway they saw that Frank had returned, with his red- haired probie in tow, and the two were chatting with Mr. and Mrs. James over a table of rocks in the backyard. The gate was open but not to worry, as Bozeman was happy enough to be in the place of his birth. He 'woofed' and wriggled happily at Jessa as she approached and he received a good ear scratching.

"What's up, Frank?" Jessa inquired of the fire chief.

"Oh, well I was just looking over your folks' treasures here! Look at this one, a beauty of a picture of a ship on the ocean, plain as day, see that? Let's look at it over here, I think the light is better for it." Motioning Jessa to come out onto the driveway with him, Frank walked around the corner of the house where her parents would not hear them.

"Oh yeah! That is a good one, Frank!" Jessa piped, then whispered "But I think the light was better where we were, so what's up?" She reiterated.

He pointed up the road to where the cable truck still sat. "You probably didn't notice those guys when you left for church since you were in a sort of a hurry." He smiled at her. "But something about them guys bothered me and it didn't occur to me until I had my belly filled." And he patted his stomach. "They're too clean, and under their uniform jackets you can see black turtlenecks poking up."

Jessa looked at him doubtfully. "Is this a crime now? Clean and wearing the same type of clothing? That's suspicious to you? I'm sorry Frank but you've lost me on this one." She shook her head.

Bozeman came up to stand by her side, then his head swung to look up the road to where the cable truck men had come out of the cab again and made as if to do some line work. The dog's ears were up, and his nose went to twitching rapidly. A low growl emanated deep from within the massive dog as he stood watching the two strange men. Jessa and Frank looked at Bozeman, then the two strangers, and at each other. "Told ya." Frank winked.

Ian and Skip approached the group, and Ian asked the question. "What's up with Bozeman?"

"I don't know, but he is not happy about those two men over there, or their equipment. It's something about them, the wrong aftershave? I haven't seen him like this about people since those two men came to our cabin looking for help. You weren't around that day, were you Ian? One had gotten his foot into a trap and needed stitching, and I drove them on the quad to your lodge and your foreman took us to town in his pickup."

"Did it leave a scar?" Ian wanted to know.

"It must have, it was pretty bad. Why? Oh, you aren't thinking these could be the same two men, that would be too weird, a one in a million or more to be sure. If it were a coincidence, I mean." Jessa stood staring at the two as if trying to convince herself of the impossibility...and yet.

CHAPTER NINETEEN

ARE YOU READY MRS. FRANKLIN?

Jessa, with Bozeman matching her every step, walked down the drive of her parent's home. Frank was at her right elbow, Ian at her left and 'Skip' trailed along behind. Bozeman kept a steady low growl emanating from within. "Heel, boy." His mistress reminded him as they approached the cable truck.

At the back of the truck the two strangers had their backs to the entourage, in hopes the group was not 'on' to them. "Doug, they are coming over. They are <u>all</u> coming over!" Dick reported as if Westfield did not already know it.

"Then it must be time to show our cards." And the six foot five inches of trained fighting machine spun around to greet them. "Good afternoon folks! Mrs. Franklin, Mr. Fuller, Chief and 'flunky', I presume." He extended his hand but pulled it back quickly when Bozeman barked and lunged at it.

"Mmm, sorry boy. I didn't mean to upset the bodyguard." But Westfield was looking straight at Ian who had stepped in between Bozeman and the stranger.

Ian peered up into the man's eyes. "How do you know us? I have never laid eyes on you before."

"Oh, but the lady knows us, don't you now ma'am? Dick, show us your pretty souvenir of our visit to the Franklin farm.

Silently Dick pulled up his pant leg and turned his leg for all to see the scar left behind by the trap. "I have wanted to say thank you for a long time, Mrs. Franklin. The hospital emergency help told me you saved me from worse and my wife appreciates that." And he smiled a little sheepish smile.

Westfield looked at Dick distastefully and his subordinate let his pant leg fall back down. Slowly they reached inside their jackets for identification. "We are United States officials and we are here to help Mrs. Franklin (Jessa gasped) to fly immediately to China to identify her husband, be he alive or dead. We have been contacted by operatives there as to the exact whereabouts of his team's exercises in plate detection and are offering you immediate transport. Are you ready, Mrs. Franklin?"

She did not like him on the sole basis that her dog wanted to tear into him, but here was a way to get to Grant and fast. "Frank, are these legitimate?" She asked of her friend while not taking her eyes off of Westfield.

Frank perused each badge individually and then compared them to each other. "They are 'legit.' Jessica. I don't trust them either, but they are official."

She shifted her gaze to Dick to ask, "Why didn't you introduce yourselves honestly before? Why sneak around like this?" And she waved her hand at the cable truck.

"It is a matter of National..." Westfield began before she cut him off.

"Not you! I asked him." Jessa reprimanded.

And Westfield's mouth temporarily hung out to dry.

Swallowing, Dick did his best to satisfy them both. "Mrs. Franklin, we cannot tell you everything, and it is classified of course." (At that he looked each person in her group in the eye.) "But we suspicion that the government of China has developed a way to actually <u>cause</u> earthquakes, and I mean in a <u>controlled</u> manner, and that your husband was about to find the key as to how they might be doing it. We think they may have caused the landslide that Mr. Franklin's team was caught up in. I am sorry to report there have not been any reports of any team member found alive."

Jessa grimaced and turned away from everyone to gather her thoughts, and wrestling her emotions into submission she asked, "Frank, do you think I should go with them?"

"Kitten, if you want to get there here is a sure fire way but I don't have a good feeling about it, no."

"Ian?" She polled.

"Absolutely not! You can't trust what they say so you can't trust what they will do."

"Skip?" She asked without looking at him.

"Me? Oh, no ma'am. I don't believe so."

"But have you ever been in love, Skip?" She asked softly without looking at him.

He hung his head and looked at his shoe before replying. "No, ma'am."

"Jessa please." Ian begged her. "Don't do this."

"You said you would go with me, but I won't hold you to it, and you and I will still be good friends." She assured him.

Ian grimaced as if in pain. "<u>Friends</u>? Is that all that we are?" And blinking he turned away.

"Look, kids." Westfield interrupted. "This is all very touching but we would like to get this show on the road, so to speak, though we will actually be spending very little time on any road. Do you get motion sickness, Mrs. Franklin? No? Very well then if you would like to follow us to the local airport we can be on our way.

"May I bring my dog?" At the off chance it were possible.

Laughing at her optimism Westfield told her "No. That does not appear to be a good idea. He may just decide to bite my ear off as I am flying us over the Pacific Ocean."

"Then I will go and say goodbye to my parents." (Wesley and Yvonne had come around to watch curiously from the middle of the driveway).

After a short and detail free explanation Jessa hugged her parents. Her mother asked her if she would please go into the house to say hello to her sister. Sighing, Jessa climbed the flight of stairs, walked down the hall to her sister's old room which was wide open, and smelled it before entering for the stench of booze like a bad perfume filled the air. She looked in upon a scene from a soap opera. There was Debra lying on her back across the width of her old bed, one arm across her stomach, the other arm hanging over the side of the bed and on the floor below it was a long, dark colored, empty bottle.

"Oh dear Lord, not again." And Jessa stepped over to her wayward sister, brushed the strand of hair away from her face then proceeded to straighten her on the bed, pull off her shoes and cover her with a blanket.

She knelt to pray. "Dear Father in heaven, You who have all knowledge can find the reason why Debra faces depression on a daily basis. You alone can lead her into great joy through forgiveness of her sins. You alone know what her sins are and you alone can forgive them. I leave her life in your guiding hands and ask that you work a miracle in her life, as she has never known. Make her know you, Father. She has tried all manner of sin, and all it has done is to make her more and more grievous, until now her parents and I fear for her very life and soul. We ask that you lay your healing hands upon her Dear Lord our Abba, our only savior. In Jesus' precious name, amen."

As Jessa raised her head, a moaning erupted from her sister and her head also lifted. "Wha's 'at noise? Who said all that? Jessica? Oh God how long have you been here?"

"About five minutes. I suppose you want me to leave?"

"Mmf...yeah. Well maybe. No, stay. Were you praying for me? You really think _that_ can help?"

"I really do know it, Deb. I know it as surely as I know the sun will rise in the morning and the stars twinkle at night, that He who made us is in control, if we will let Him. Do you remember the song we used to sing in church school? Sing it with me. "Jesus loves me, this I know, for the bible tells me so. Little ones to Him belong, they are weak, but He is strong..."

For a moment Debra started to hum along. "Stop it! I am not like you, Jessica! I'm not strong!" She cried aloud. "You can stand alone and not be lonely! I can't! I've tried, but I can't do it! What's wrong with me? Why won't a man stay with me?" And she fell to blubbering tears into the bedspread.

Jessa stood and looked around the room, then went to searching it. She uncovered a dusty bible that she had given to her sister years ago. Blowing a layer of dust off of it she handed it down to Debra on the bed, stating, "Here is my strength, and you can have it too." And surprising even herself Jessa bent low and kissed the top of Debra's head before leaving the room.

Downstairs she found her parents, and Ian being introduced to Freddy in the fishbowl. "He must be pretty old, then!" He was saying to Yvonne. He looked up at the sound of Jessa's boots coming down the stairs. "But he looks so young, do you feed him something special because he looks great!"

"Oh no, he is a special little guy though." Yvonne looked away from him to ask her daughter. "Jessica, was Debra awake?"

She is now mom. Don't worry mom; I was nice. So, I will see you guys in about a week or two, I guess. I really don't know. I love you both." And she hugged both of her parents one last time before heading for the door.

Ian tailed her.

"Ian, I will take you to the airport and you can get a flight back home." She told him after the screen door closed behind them.

"What? Why are you trying to get rid of me? How can you suddenly turn me away? Is it because you only needed me to help you get this far and now you have someone who can fly you the rest of the way?" He whispered painfully, "Have you been using me?"

Jessa stopped dead in her tracks and turned to face him. "I will do whatever I have to do to find my husband. But where I have to go is an unstable place and I don't want to put you in danger, unnecessary danger."

Her voice quavered with her own words as the reality of the last few minutes sank in and overwhelmed her being.

Ian came closer. "Jessa I love you. I may be just a friend, but one that will go to the ends of the earth for you, with you. If Grant is alive and you leave me in China, then I must be happy that your dream has come true. I will be coming to the airport not to fly home to Canada, but to accompany you and do whatever those two space cadets come up with."

She laughed back her tears at his analogy of the two men at the cable truck, who were watching them right now. Had not

Frank and 'Skip' been keeping them company they would be eavesdropping on the conversation at the Suburban via their electronic listening devices hidden away inside the truck.

"Alright my dearest friend, let's do this thing together." She gave his hands a squeeze and together they climbed into the Flyer and waved to Frank and 'Skip' as they followed the cable truck to the airport.

CHAPTER TWENTY

NO FLIGHT PATTERN

The two vehicles arrived at the airport and after checking in at the gate Westfield told the saluting guard "And they are with us." as he thumbed at the Flyer. They had bypassed the terminal and gone to the hangars to drive to the farthest building.

Dick got out to unlock the rollaway door and push it open, then trotted inside and the cable truck followed. Westfield drove slowly around the massive helicopter to the very end of the hangar. The Flyer entered also, its passengers in awe of the mighty machine.

Westfield came up to Jessa's door to open it and proceeded to open the other doors as well. He grabbed her duffle bag but left the guitar case, and Ian's things as well. Escorting her into the helicopter he set foot to enter, then swung around to meet Ian face to face. He was laden with luggage and ready to enter as well.

"What do you think you are doing?" Westfield demanded of him.

"Like you said before, I'm the bodyguard." Ian smirked at him.

Dick had set the engines to start/run and the overhead blades began to move.

Westfield queried of Jessa "Mrs. Franklin, is <u>this</u> (and he jerked a thumb at Ian) something you want along?"

Sizing the situation she stated firmly "I won't go with you without him."

Douglas Westfield Commander of Special Forces stood aside so that Ian Fuller could enter the copter, then he shut and locked the door and proceeded forward to set coordinates to their first refueling site, as Dick familiarized their passengers with the chairs they would be sitting in for the next eleven hours.

"Straps come down over the head and around your waist, like so." He 'clicked' the belt shut. "If you feel sleepy or simply need a change of position, this lever." And Jessa's seat spread out into a lounge chair and tilted back, and a lever locked it all into place. Dick continued "Now if you want, your feet can slip into these rings so that they won't fall out if we should take a sudden turbulent drop while you are asleep!" He reported proudly of his own design.

Ian had followed suit and each were locked into the contours of the seats, then helmets fitted to their heads made them ready for flight. Dick joined Westfield at the controls and together they went through the preflight check. A loud humming ensued and the great 'bird' lifted off the ground and spun around to face forward before leaving the hangar. Dick radioed the gate that the hangar door was ready to close and lock, and they were on their way. Climbing higher and higher into the sky roared the black thunderous machine with its four passengers.

Jessa was aware of a nauseating feeling growing in the pit of her stomach, fortunately it eased as they leveled off and flew less dramatically. Looking over at Ian however, she was surprised at how sweaty he looked. She gave him a supportive smile but the chopper was so loud she feared any words would have to be shouted, although she saw that the pilots had intercom in their helmets and could speak freely without having to yell.

From where Jessa and Ian sat they could not see the city of Bozeman growing smaller beneath them as they plunged through the sky far above, they could not see Frank pointing at them for 'Skip' and saying "There they go!" They could not hear Debra wiping her sniffles as she turned pages in her bible and asked mom and dad how they "came to believe all this stuff? And what does it mean, 'only begotten son', anyway?"

All they could see was that they were moving at great speed in a vehicle of a type they had never known existed before this very hour. This helicopter was made for extensive trips, had several kinds of special tracking devices outside and in and was capable of refueling in the air. It was more enclosed than any that either one of them had seen, for it was also an office/portable command post, as well as a flying gunnery. There was a clock showing all the time zones of the world, locked drawers labeled: "Geographical/Topographical", "Weather Maps/Jet Stream Fluctuations/Airline Routes", "Tectonic Plates/ Fault Lines/Statistical Probabilities", "Satellite locator & Rotation Times/ Orbital Flux /Tides /Moon", and an inset computer screen and keyboard, wand and mouse stuck by Velcro to a pad above a clear case of discs, for the more specialized, classified technologies.

Ian had closed his eyes to pray. Jessa thought it a most appropriate thing to do considering the circumstances and followed suit. A minute later when she looked across at him the sweaty look had vanished and he smiled back at her and reached out for her hand. Eventually it did not seem like such an unnatural thing to be zooming above the clouds at hundreds of miles an hour, destination danger if even they survived the journey, for they had each other for strength and comfort.

As they were flying west and at great speed the sun stayed up longer than it would have if they had stayed on the ground, but even man's mighty abilities cannot keep up with God's creation, and so the sun did slowly set as they crossed high above the Oregon border and over the Pacific ocean shoreline.

Jessa's hand slipped out of Ian's grasp as they both had fallen asleep somewhere hundreds of miles north of Hawaii, and that far south of the Aleutian Islands, when suddenly the chopper took a sharp dive and woke them from their reclining position, which immediately had them looking down at the pilots, one of which had also been asleep. It was Westfield who was grinning over at a shocked from sleep Dick, and had purposely nose- dived the copter on a lark.

"Doug! That's not funny! Especially with civilians on

board!" But his specially designed seats had done their jobs commendably so that Jessa and Ian were intact, though somewhat ruffled.

The aircraft leveled somewhat.

"Are you crazy?" Ian demanded. "Set this thing down right now so I can rip your head off!"

Westfield responded wordlessly by dropping altitude again, showing them the living ocean rising up to greet them.

Ian squirmed in his seat. "I meant on the ground!"

Westfield laughed and reached for the radio 'mic.' "Sub Base Two Command, Sub Base Two Command, this is Air One Command, do you copy?" There was a short pause.

"Air One Command, this is Sub Base Two Command, we copy you and are ready, willing and able to comply with your order to refuel. Commencing docking pad procedure. You may extend your hose coupling."

Westfield complied with buttons on the panel to his left. If the passengers had unbuckled and walked to the front where the wrap around windows allowed viewing, they could have seen a lone platform rising up out of the sea by way of a hydraulic ram pushing its way upward from the hidden submarine below the surface. They were able to feel the "thud" as the airbase barely fit atop the platform and automatic steel rings held it in place. The pilot did not power down, for one never knew when an extra large swell would wash over the platform and they might need an emergency takeoff.

They had been six hours in the chopper so far. "May we have a break?" Jessa tried not to sound as if she were begging. "Is there a commode?"

Westfield told Dick to handle it while he would oversee the fueling.

"Ahem." Dick began as he helped her to disengage the lock on her seat. "Here it is." And he pulled from a cabinet a slide out seat over a bucket and showed her how to flush. Dick went forward again and busied himself with looking out the window, and Ian made sure of it as he stood guard for her. Having finished, she used a disposable moist towelette from the dispenser and tossed it in as per the instructions on the packet. Jessa returned to her seat area, then ventured forward to watch the dark swaying sea and try to imagine the submarine full of people below them, somewhere, but she could see no clue of them from under the rippling, swaying water.

Each man in turn did use the commode before chemicals were added to the holding tank to cause instant dissolution of waste. They each were given a large bar of condensed energy supplying grains and dried fruit, a bottle of water and a square of chewing gum formulated to clean teeth of plaque. Efficiency was prime in this type of isolated command post.

"Saddle up, people!" Westfield boomed. "We have spent our allotment of twenty minutes already. The next half of our little excursion will prove more interesting I am sure."

Wondering how that could possibly be, Jessa and Ian relocked their seats as the hose coupling disengaged from the platform outlet, and the engine roared to full power at the same moment the steel bindings released them into the sky. Once they were away, the platform retracted under the surface and the submarine dropped its depth once more, to wait.

Rising higher and still higher the great machine thrust their bodies toward space until the visitors feared they may never stop rising. Finally they leveled off and Ian and Jessa could breathe again without such tremendous effort. This time Dick took over the controls while Westfield tilted his seat back and made as if to sleep. In another four hours they would be flying over China's waters and into their air space, then he would take up the controls once more.

Flying above the clouds it was a beautiful starlit night, Jessa could see that much at least. The lights had long since been dimmed inside the copter and soon enough they would be traveling through blackness outside as well. She knew Dick had been guiding the craft by the stars, his compass, and constantly checking radar for any air traffic. There was none within a hundred miles in any direction as this was not a touring vessel making its way upon a popular route.

They had experienced air turbulence more than a few

times since Montana, enough to where she grew accustomed to a sudden drop in altitude or a scary shuddering of the pitch control mechanism, or rotator blades, from above. Obviously it was nothing unusual to the pilots.

"Jessa." She heard Ian call to her and she looked away from the stars.

"I'm sorry I lost my cool back there, when Westfield was showing off, I mean. I will try to do better next time, and I <u>know</u> there will be a next time." He grimaced.

"I know you will. It's all this sudden surreal business that has us off guard!" She shouted back and smiled at him, then held out her hand and within a few minutes they were asleep, hands drifting apart but hearts intertwined.

CHAPTER TWENTYONE

CROSSING THE DATELINE

Flying high over the International Dateline, and a few short hours later, or so it seemed to a sleeping Douglas Westfield, Dick tapped him to take over the controls while he concentrated strictly on radar detection. Westfield reset his chair to the upright position, rubbed his face and took the controls. Checking their position he quietly ordered into the headset "Silent running, and pass the word to them, there is to be no sound from here on in."

"Aye sir." Dick spoke softly into his intercom and released his seatbelt to wake the passengers for a briefing.

Shaking them gently, Dick alerted Jessa and Ian that from this point on they were not to speak or move about, and it would be best if they sat up in their chairs so as not to be stirring about with metal locks and buckles later on. Nodding, they obeyed and sat uprightly, 'clicking' the locks into place. All set, but for what? They did not know.

Westfield had initiated the radar blocking devices on the outside of the helicopter so that they were cloaked from detection. Also their speed necessarily decreased and a softer sound emanated from the whirling blades. On any radar they may have been confused with a tightly knit flock of geese. In another hour they were over China's waters, though the passengers were not aware of it, and soon over land. In forty-five minutes more there was a 'blip' on Dick's tracking screen. He tapped Westfield and pointed to it. His commander nodded approval and veered slightly to compensate for drift, then dropped altitude at a steady pace indicative to a flock of geese landing on a high mountain lake, although birds would not normally be in flight this long before sunrise. As it came nearer the surface of the lake the great metal bird seemingly veered into a mountainside, then could be heard no more.

From inside the mountain cave, men clad in dark turtleneck sweaters, black pants and boots dropped a dark camouflage curtain over the entrance. Standard issue were their black belts and black watches, neither of which would the sun glint a reflection off of had there been any sun.

The helicopter's four passengers 'clicked' loose and slowly rose up from their confinements to stretch and shake out the stiffness of their ordeal.

Westfield sized them up, one by one, then decided, "Well done, Dick!" Then looking at the 'civies', "Surprisingly well done." He frowned at having to rethink his judgments of them, although perhaps they could pull this thing off after all. "Let's roll!" He yelled at his company and all four exited the mighty chopper, she followed her destiny and Ian followed his heart's desire.

Following the Commander to a jeep, Jessa was directed to put on first a desert 'camo' raincoat then a matching life vest over top, and sit next to him in the front. Ian climbed in the back to don his issued coat and vest but Dick stayed behind with the chopper while another soldier climbed in next to Ian and quietly the jeep rolled out between the camouflage and into the rainy night. Onto a narrow mountain road, which dropped altitude immediately, winding around and down for two miles to a level below the lake where a small mountain stream grew into a creek, and the rain flooded creek became a small rushing river, the jeep quietly crept along.

At a point in the river they stopped and Westfield and the other soldier got out to lift tree branches and bushes out of the way, revealing a dark canoe and paddles. The soldier hopped back into the jeep and drove away, back up the mountain and to the cave.

To Westfield's bidding Ian took an end of the canoe, and together they carried the thing to the rushing water. Commander Westfield motioned for Jessa to sit in the middle and hold the tiny lantern low in the boat, barely above the edge so that they could see for a short distance in front of them. There were no seats and so Ian settled on his knees at the front with a paddle, then Douglas himself pushed off and stepped in, settling himself down on his knees as well, to steer from the stern with his paddle. They went with the current, this way and that, Ian would push them away from any logs or debris getting in the way and this went on until nearly sunrise. Then it was time to pull over and tie off. Dowsing the dim light, Westfield dug out a duffle bag of his own and pulled out two small breathing tanks with masks.

Water went rushing all around them and still trickled from the sky above as he spoke only loudly enough for them to hear him, and explain. "I was not expecting you to bring a bodyguard, Mrs. Franklin." Westfield smirked at Ian. "So I only have two of these things and it will be best if you and I share one in the culvert we are about to grope our way through, and I am sorry but it will be a rough go. There is enough air in each of these for ten minutes. I am adept at functioning under oxygen stressed conditions and that is how I am making my decision that you share with me. All you have to do is hold onto me and give me a gulp of air about every half minute, can you do that?" He asked of Jessa. She nodded her understanding as Ian grimaced at the thought. He continued "We need to remove our life vests now for ease of movement, do you both swim?" They nodded. "Good! Maybe that will save me having to search for your bodies before a westerner can be discovered on these shores." He said it without joking.

Westfield turned his attention to Ian. "Fuller, we will be pulling hand over hand our way through a large culvert under the road that reaches up to a hospital's backdoor service entrance. The current will be strong and filled with debris from flooding, so pull your hood down and tie it on tight, that and your mask will be your only form of protection. You will not be able to see anything so don't try, it would only distract you. You may lose your sense of direction, so keep your arms working at pulling above your head, that will be a reminder of which way is up. Don't try to use your feet by hooking your boots into the wire mesh, there is not room for a toehold and it may cause you to lose track of my position and even your grip, and you will be swept away! And if that happens once you <u>might</u> catch up again, but if it happens twice you <u>will</u> run out of air before commanding the opening. Do you understand?"

Ian nodded grimly as Westfield secured the mask onto his face, and as he saw the soldier place Jessa's arm around his neck as they submerged, he struggled to secure his emotions in check as well.

CHAPTER TWENTYTWO

DON'T GO IN THERE!

As they submerged, Westfield put Jessa's arms about his neck and had her practice breathing into the tank's handheld cup for air, and then transferring it to him. He breathed, nodded to her, and she took it back to her own mouth to hold for thirty seconds before sharing again.

Then they were gone into the torrent, and Ian followed. Inside the culvert Westfield placed Jessa between himself and the concrete pipe that was lined with a type of woven wire that was somewhat stronger than her chicken coup fencing. Its intention was not so that operatives from another country could sneak their way through an unprecedented flood and enter a hospital in the predawn hour, but it worked. The water was horrendous but Jessa was able to hang on to Westfield's neck with one arm and alternate the air tank with the other as he pulled the two of them along through the raging current. She did not try to open her eyes for she had no mask as the men did, she kept her head under his, on his chest, and the durable hood of the raincoat made a fair helmet.

Westfield was concentrating on finding the next handhold and ducking debris as it seemed to fly past them. He was nearly certain there would be little danger from actual trees coming into this flusher as it was high above the river, but there could be no guarantee. He would protect his charge in any way possible. She was certainly a surprise to have come this far, that is, no screaming or crying had she emitted even though he had roughly tested her, and he did know how to test people. That Fuller back there, he was all right too, except he is after another man's wife, if Franklin *is* alive that is, he countered himself. This would all be so much easier if Franklin would simply show up dead, end of crisis. But now he had to coerce the man's wife to come to China under false pretenses of identifying him, as if a D.N.A. match and their entire collection of photo Id.s' of the man would not be enough. But if he were found alive, and had knowledge of their weather manipulations, they may need a bargaining chip to shut him up. He felt the oxygen drain on his system when at that moment a rubber mouthpiece fit over his lips. Expelling the last bit of air in his lungs in order to push the mucky water out of the cup before using it to breathe, Douglas Westfield inhaled like a hungry baby on a bottle. He appreciated her attention to timing and detail; she made a better breathing partner than Dick had proven to be. Was there light up ahead? Were they almost to the end? It could not come too soon for any of them. He wondered how Fuller was doing.

Ian had started off right behind them, but then he lost equilibrium for a time and had traveled around the culvert a bit instead of proceeding straight up it. Now he was several precious seconds behind, his injured shoulder screaming in pain and his breathing indicated a panic attack.

The sun was about to rise, and all around the excavation site down below them soldiers could be seen arriving to relieve those who had worked through the night, searching for victims lost in the mud.

A few more feet, two more, one more hand reach and "Gasp!" Westfield's head was the first to emerge from the wide hole, and he pulled Jessa up and pushed her onto the embankment before pulling himself up out of the culvert. "Get down!" He warned with an urgent whisper and rolled over on top of her as a truck laden with supplies headed up the mucky road to the hospital. No one in the truck noticed the desert 'camo.' covered with mud as everything else these days was covered with mud.

Westfield watched them go, and then looked around

briefly before peering down into Jessa's eyes. He felt her shivering beneath him. "I've got to get you inside."

She nodded agreement with chattering teeth. "B-b-b- but wh- wh- where is Ian?" She feared for her friend.

"He will be along soon enough." Westfield stated confidently and put one arm around her back and the other under her legs and lifted.

"No!" She refused to leave Ian behind. "He must be in t- t- trouble, we have to help him! I'll go back, th- th- there's enough air left for me!"

He looked in wonder at her featherweight frame struggling in his arms. It was no effort at all for him to restrain her, and yet he could not allow her to suffer this grief needlessly. "Stay here." He sighed as he set her back down on the mud. Breathing in deeply and quickly in order to fill his lungs, he slipped back down into the gushing water and out of sight. "I can't believe I'm doing this." He thought. He entered the culvert at high speed with his legs spread apart and his torso twisted with arms at length. A man would not slip through such a design undetected and almost immediately Douglas had hold on a confused and panicking Ian. Doug took hold of Ian's face, and pressing their masks together he saw it, terror. He kept his own eyes focused on Fuller's until sanity found its way back into them, then relief, and the two men could proceed up and out of the culvert.

Gasping for air, they worked their way to the embankment and threw themselves at Jessa's feet. She pulled Ian up onto the embankment to lay panting and retching next to her, and then and much to the commander's surprise, she returned for Doug. She cried tears of gratitude to God, and to Douglas for saving her dear companion. "Come on, there's no time for that now." Westfield reminded them.

Crawling on slippery mud in the cold wet darkness, Douglas Westfield Commander of Air- Base One and Sub- Base Two, trainer of soldiers elite, felt something underneath his frigid, soaking wet turtleneck that he had counted as dead and buried long ago; a warm glow? Naw, it couldn't be, he told himself as he again scooped up this shivering, soaking featherweight and headed for the hospital's delivery entrance, with a heaving, panting Ian trailing closely behind.

They had to wait in the bushes until the truck had left after depositing its delivery of medicines before they could enter undetected, to hide in the uniform closet/laundry room where Douglas found what they needed.

A bag marked in Chinese that spelled out "To be burned" lay tucked away behind a washing machine. He pulled it out of its place of refuge and opened it. Inside were clean towels, which he doled out to his companions, then handed a small wrapped pile of ladies clothes to Jessa and larger ones for himself and Ian. They were Red Cross uniforms, enhanced with black turtleneck sweaters to wear underneath, and name tags with each person's picture.

Jessa rinsed out her hair in the washtub, dislodging bits of grass and chunks of mud, while wishing she could climb into the basin and take a full bath, but this was not the time. Ian held one of the large white towels out, as a curtain for Jessa to change behind, which also afforded Douglas some privacy, not that he cared so much. Then Jessa turned to face the wall of the small room so that Ian could put on dry clothes. The sweaters were wonderfully warm, and <u>finally</u> the shivering stopped. When Douglas reached into the magic bag one last time, out came the energy bars and water bottles. Frantically they tore off the wrappers and ate without speaking. They drank the water thirstily and chewed their gum as before, and each thought of the adventure they were caught up in and how suddenly their own opinions of the others had changed since the first time they had dined on these very rations. At last they were finished and somewhat refreshed, ready to go on.

Jessa had wished for a shower, shampoo, rinse and blow dry, but those things had not found their way into the bag. She pulled the drawstring from it and deftly tied her wet hair back and up into a ponytail, then wrapped it all up and into a bun.

The door to the washroom opened and the three operatives emerged. Walking abreast up the hallway the three now looked as if they belonged there, and they were able to relax somewhat, even Ian was over the heaves of the culvert trauma. They came around a corner to view what looked like a waiting room that had been transformed into a triage unit, for on the usual couches and chairs were dozens of battered and bloodied would be patients waiting their turn to get treatment. These were people with no hope of actually seeing a doctor for there were so many in greater need, and those were the ones squeezed into an actual room upstairs.

After checking each face from a distance the three foreigners took the stairwell to the second floor to search for other hospital workers who might know of an American geologist pulled from the rubble. No one knew of him on the second floor, and so they took the stairs to the third floor. It was on the fourth floor that Jessa could have been knocked down with a feather when she realized the two volunteers in the hallway speaking to a lovely Chinese girl were her own in laws. Bess and Don Franklin were in a tight huddle with what appeared to be a local hospital volunteer in a white lab coat, when the three strangers entered the hallway.

Jessa stopped dead in her tracks with her mouth wide open. Douglas noticed it first and nudged her, asking "Someone you know?"

"Uh huh." She nodded and her eyes became moist before she could cry out. "Bess, Don! It's Jessa!" And she began to run down the hallway toward them.

Curiously the Chinese girl ran away from her and entered another room through two glass doors marked by the Red Cross in English "Urgent Care."

Bess opened her arms for Jessa to hug her with all the might left in her. Don put his long, lanky arms around the two women and hugged them as his eyes dripped tears of joy at seeing the great love his daughter in law had for his son, that she would come all this way for him in this great time of need. He noticed the two men standing behind her and alerted Bess, "Looks like Jessica isn't alone, dear."

Bess studied the men and her daughter in law. "Jessa dear, may we speak to you alone?" She asked while taking steps away from the men.   Jessa stammered. "I, I guess so Bess, but whatever you have to say..." Then she stopped talking so she could listen to a vaguely familiar voice coming from somewhere. Yes, it was coming from behind those same doors the Chinese girl had dashed into, she thought as her hand reached for one of the knobs.

Bess cried out "No Jessa! Don't go in there!"

But too late, for the voice had been a magnet to Jessa's very soul, it spoke to her of a deep longing, it was the culmination of every effort and energy spent since she had left home to find him. The voice had changed somehow. It was hoarse and raspy as if it had been screaming for long hours, and yet it was the same.

Opening the door Jessa beheld her husband, and like her, he also wore a white coat. The Chinese girl was holding him by the shoulders as if to keep him from something. He looked back at Jessa with a look of desperation and confusion. Then Mai-Ling looked away from Jessa and took Grant's face in her hands to kiss him hard and long.

Jessa's hands flew up to hide her eyes as she screamed, but then fell limply for she had fainted away.

Ian caught her up before she could hit the floor and he lay her on the only remaining empty cot. The patient inhabiting it had died minutes before of her many wounds, and the corpse brought to the morgue for identification and family notification. The room was filled with other cots in a row against each wall and down the middle, all were full of beaten bodies, some moaning while others lay unconscious.

Ian spun around to glare at Grant then walked toward him with accusations flying.

Grant did not move away but was shaking all over and not only because he was certain his nose was about to be broken.

Mai-Ling stepped in front of Grant as if to protect him. "Please suh, do not hurt our doctor!" She begged with eyes wide.

Then Douglas Westfield filled Ian's vision. "That will be enough, Fuller."

But Ian pushed past Douglas, saying "Oh, no. He has it coming for what he's done to Jessa! The nightmares she's had, the agony of not knowing. The children she has wanted but been denied! A life of happiness that you have denied her!" He yelled at Grant.

Douglas jumped in again with "Ian, you may be right. He may very well deserve it, but this will have to wait."

"Get out of my way, Westfield!" Ian's steady gaze burned hot.

"Stand down, Fuller!" Douglas replied earnestly.

Ian's right arm pulled back with his torso following, then reversed action, building power as his fist came flying back and pushing forward, and through thin air for the soldier had squatted in that moment and rolled back to bring his feet up and onto Ian's chest which was already in forward motion, and that energy was used to lift and roll him onto the floor. Douglas could have kicked Ian over several beds, yet it was a hospital and he knew this man was not his enemy. Douglas meant only to purge his opponent's anger before he could damage the very man they were here to find, and interrogate.

His shoulder throbbed in pain, but Ian was up again and heading for Grant once more. Mai-Ling had an inspiration and grabbed the geologist by the hand to half drag him to Jessa's bedside to use as a sanctuary. Bess and Don followed her lead, and Grant found himself defended by his mother, father, cohort, and unconscious wife on a cot. He looked down at her and suffered that he must not even say her name. Would he ever be able to win her forgiveness? He reached out to hold her hand on pretense of taking a pulse.

"Don't you touch her, Kent!" Ian screamed, and then realized what he had said. Blinking and shaking his head, Ian turned away from his anger to meet with his grief. Somehow, he knew he had lost again.

Douglas was not quite sure why the fight was suddenly over, but he was glad not to have to brake and bloody this man he had begun to like. He watched as Ian leaned against a wall, and then slumped to the floor.

Staying between him and the group at the cot, Douglas ventured, "Mr. Franklin, what have you been up to?" And he showed Grant and the others his badge.

CHAPTER TWENTYTHREE

KEEPING SECRET

"Jessa dear, please wake up!" Bess patted Jessa's cheek with her hand.

Opening her fluttering eyelids ever so slightly Jessa recognized her mother in law, then closed her lids again, squeezing out the tears. "I don't want to wake up, ever." And she turned her face away only to find Don standing there.

After checking everyone's whereabouts: Mr. Westfield was questioning his son as Grant checked his patients' Iv. bags, and Mai- Ling had shyly gone to Mr. Fuller with these very words while Don bent low to whisper them above Jessa's ear. "Things are not what they seem, Jessica. Take heart in that. He loves you, but he cannot show it right now or..." and Don stopped abruptly when Bess, whose eyes had not strayed from Mr. Westfield's whereabouts, shushed him.

Douglas came over with concern on his face for Jessa. "How are you holding up now, kid? I did not expect to see you knocked down like this, not after all I have seen you do and go through to get here. The thing is, your husband has selective amnesia. He has skills in healing he picked up who knows when, I guess all of you folks do?"

And Don related how Grant and Jessa had met as 'E.M.T.' s on the Bozeman fire department.

"Ah, I see." Douglas responded. "But Grant does not realize that. He was injured in the landslide and took a bump on his head. He remembers being brought here in a jeep by a soldier and Mai-Ling here." And Douglas swung a hand out toward the young woman talking quietly with Ian. She solemnly looked over at the group around the cot, then back to Ian and he nodded to her as if in agreement over something, then raised himself up off the floor and together they walked around the middle row of cots toward Grant.

Douglas watched them for any signs of animosity. There were none. The two men shook hands for a long moment. "Well, she is quite the little peacemaker! She should be in politics." Douglas judged unwittingly.

"Douglas..." Jessa begged and the commander's head spun back around as if he thought a foe had entered the room, "would you take me home, please?" A tear rolled down her cheek.

Wiping the tear away with his thumb, Douglas cleared his throat, then pulled a compact radio from inside his Red Cross jacket and held it to his mouth. "Dick, we have enough information here. Affirmative, I will have everybody on the roof at twenty two hundred hours for a scoop and go operation. Roger that and thanks, Westfield out. Good enough, 'kitten'?" He asked with a self-assured wink.

Surprised that he had adopted Frank's pet nickname for her, Jessa looked at him quizzically.

He answered her look with "You can be pretty darn tough, yet weak as a kitten, and all because of him." Douglas threw a look at Grant. "I think you will have all your prayers answered, all in good time. Did that just come out of me?" He shook his head. "You must be influencing me." He smiled and looked away.

A few minutes ago Jessa thought she would never smile again, but a faint one played at her lips just now. "Thank you for all you have done, Douglas, you are an extraordinary man."

He sobered. "All in the line of duty, ma'am."

She sat up on the cot at last, and offered him her hand. He took it to pull her into him and held her there without struggle. He commanded the attention of the room now. "If these other two bozos don't work out, I will find out about it and come looking for you. If they don't treat you right I will know and come looking for them!" Then he did the unimaginable and kissed her forehead for all to see, and looking directly at Grant, he winked.

Jessa did not see the wink but did feel the color rise to her cheeks and she excused herself to find the restroom. Mai-Ling offered to show her the way and Jessa stiffly accepted, then Bess decided she could go as well.

Douglas counted the minutes until they returned. Seventeen must be too long, he thought and headed for the doors to go looking for them when in they walked.

Jessa felt more anxious than ever over Grant, though she did not dare come close to him for fear the secret she now shared would become clear. Also she and Ian could not exchange glances without fearing Douglas was taking note of it.

Bess and Don were adept at helping Grant with the patients, Mai-Ling would jot down notes on her clipboard as she followed him along. She was capable of translating English instructions into Chinese, or from Chinese to English. "So, what will you do about him?" Douglas asked Jessa and nodded at Grant. "You know he thinks he is engaged to that squinty-eyed girl. She even seems to believe it. She says her father wanted them to marry. That sounds pretty bad. And he does not even remember being your husband, the idiot. Isn't that grounds for leaving him here?" He asked, with one eyebrow raised high.

An hour ago Jessa would have adamantly disagreed. Then twenty minutes ago she had wanted to ask, "How soon can we leave?" But now, after her debriefing in the restroom, "I have prayed many times that I would find him alive, and that prayer has been miraculously answered. As for the rest, he needs a doctor, a psychologist, maybe. But I need to get him away from here, away from his point of trauma. Is it possible to bring him out with us?" She asked of him.

Studying her, Douglas responded "What about the girl? She won't want to leave without knowing the fate of her father, but she is engaged. You of all people know how strong that bond is."

At that, Jessa raised her eyebrows together and gave him a hopeful look.

Leaning closer and whispering, Douglas Westfield wanted to know one thing. "Do you think Air Base One is a taxicab for your personal will?"

And at her fallen demeanor and reply "Oh, I overstepped. I apologize. You probably have a more important mission lined up, in Iraq, or someplace exotic."

Straightening now Westfield's hand went ever so slowly inside his jacket and once again pulled out his two-way radio. "Dick? Westfield here, pull out the Velcro hammocks, we have two more sleepers for the slumber party. Just do it. Roger, twenty two hundred hours is still a go, Westfield out." He checked his watch. "Well, eleven hours to make like I belong here; better make myself useful." And Douglas Westfield set himself to changing soiled cots and doing laundry, then scrounged up trays of food for every worker in the Urgent Care section of the fourth floor. Now and then he would visit with each member of his group of interest to see if any of them had changed any part of their story. They held fast to their previous words, so much so that he saw a pattern.

Douglas had left it to Jessa to inform Don and Bess that Grant and Mai- Ling could leave for home "Tonight!" And Jessa left it to them to convince Grant and Mai- Ling.

"So, my chance to go to America comes today, but at what cost?"

Mai- Ling spoke in a melancholy mood. But she nodded her agreement to Bess.

Don caught up Grant's attention away from a bloodied man he had been bandaging. "Son," he whispered, "Mai- Ling has agreed, that even though there is still no word of her father, to come away tonight. Mr. Westfield has a way to take you home, son. Your mother and I will return as planned with A.D.R.A. in ten days, we owe them that. I hope you will wait at our house or the James' home until we arrive. We would like to see you again under better circumstances." Don smiled meekly at his son. He ached to hug him again but ever since the United States government had come through those doors, he dared not.

Grant told his dad "These people need attention, but I will

leave with Mai-Ling, Mr. Franklin. Tell your superiors before I leave tonight that we need one more level four 'E.M.T.' up here. Even if I stayed, I cannot go on much longer without rest, I just can't do it." And he turned his attention to the next moaning patient.

Similar hours passed in short conversations. Jessa helped clean the new arrivals before they received their bandages, injections, 'Iv.'s. She found a mop and disinfectant and took to shining the muddied linoleum while Ian and Douglas scrubbed the walls and fixtures, and before ten o'clock came they could feel good about leaving these poor people with a better place than when they had arrived, though it was a small compensation for taking Grant away from them. That thought left Jessa feeling a little guilty in a place of such great need and by so very many, for she was only one.

But the time did come to go and as they were saying their 'goodbye's to Bess and Don and heading for the doors, a muddied soldier came running with news for Mai-Ling. "Cousin! We have found your father's body! We may put him to rest now. Please don't cry so. Remember his happiness for you in your new life. It is as he wished it, you honor him with your courage." The young man gave her a small but heavy metal frame. It folded in the middle and closed with a latch. "We found this on his person, Mai-Ling. You must keep it now."

She opened it and saw an old picture of herself as a young school girl, with her happy parents, one on each side of her, still years before her mother would be killed. "You honor me with your thoughtfulness, I will miss you Tai!" And she hugged him, muddy coat and all.

"Let's go, people!" And Westfield herded his flock to the hospital roof, leaving Tai to go back to the digging.

They opened the door into the windy darkness and stood expectantly.

In that moment it took their eyes to grow accustomed to the black night, they collectively gasped at the realization that a mighty helicopter stood before them. No one had heard a sound or felt a vibration as it landed, accolades to Dick's abilities.

Jessa urged Grant and a timid Mai- Ling to follow Commander Westfield into the metal bird, and then she and Ian followed. As they neared the door and saw Dick step up to help first Mai- Ling then Grant and escort them to the rear, Ian stepped in front of her, saying "I may never get to do this again." And hugged Jessa silently as if to say goodbye.

They parted and climbed inside to hear Dick explaining to Grant how to slide his seat out if he so chose to do so later. "But for right now, stay upright until we are out of Chinese territory, I will let you know when." He said soberly. "Mr. Fuller, nice to see you again, do you remember the chair? Show me please? Very good, helmets everyone!" And Dick handed the men each a helmet, then he turned to the two women standing behind him.

Jessa saw that this time there were two hammock-type cages hanging down above the men. They were made of black woven strapping and bolted to the ceiling and upper walls a mere two feet above Grant and Ian. She was getting an uneasy feeling when Dick's narration referred to these trappings. "You ladies, being the lightest and shortest of the group, will be riding in these. Ordinarily we use them for equipment. Please put your helmets on, here you go. Now step up here onto the foothold of the chair, that's it, and set your bottom in first, Mrs. Franklin. Lie back and take this end of the strap here. See the hook? It goes up top and with a 'click' you are locked in." Then it was Mai- Ling's turn and reluctantly she became the second bird in a gilded cage.

Douglas had started the engines and after a momentary preflight check they lifted off as quietly as a fruit bat, only this one was loaded with radar blocking devices for secret flight.

Jessa heard a loud "gasp!" from Mai- Ling at the moment of liftoff, for the two young women lay side by side in their swings. Mai- Ling had never flown in anything before, and these were not ideal conditions by any means conducive to confidence. Jessa snuck a peek at her long sought- after husband, who in spite of everything covert he had been swept up into, lay fast asleep.

Grant's last few days had been a grueling ordeal of pain and grief, stirred with guilt. But even before that there had been a growing apprehension that his government had somehow created a weapon of enormous potential. He had seen it in his probe's satellite feedback readouts, mysterious atmospheric vibrations that had systematic patterns, unnatural patterns. He had tapped into satellites from all countries of the world and yet only those bearing "United States of America" insignia had caused his geo-graphs to be covered in these patterns. And only in cases of freakish weather had they occurred, such as in this particular province of China whose rain had only now abated, coincidentally as they were leaving after having recovered the last corpse of his team and he himself was in the grasp of the rainmakers.

As a scientist Grant had learned early to be wary of anything termed coincidental. He had proven to the world that tectonic plates slide for a reason and not mere coincidence or fate, as some would believe.

Now he must prove that weather manipulation is a false hope of those who would rule the planet. It will only cause chaos where there was once a semblance of order. The earth's supply of useable precipitation is nonnegotiable; the amount is finite and yes can be coerced into dumping into one place rather than dispersed over many. But herein lies the problem, the many other continents that will suffer over the win of a country to a certain union through weather oppression. Oppression to one will be depression to many. In the end all will suffer, and will they be flexible enough, intelligent enough, strong and quick enough to survive? He must stop it somehow. And that is why Westfield and others like him must not know that he, Grant Franklin, is 'on' to them. Grant's musings from under his eyelids ended with "At least Jessa knows I am still alive, but will we ever be able to have the life we dreamed of?" And Grant drifted off to sleep below his wife.

CHAPTER TWENTYFOUR

STANDOFF

"Leaving the Red Zone, sir." Dick informed his commander, who in turn caused the radar blocking devices to retract so that their speed increased, as well as the noise level.

Commander Westfield took a long look at their passengers. "All asleep?" He queried of Dick, and more than a bit surprised.

"Aye sir. Mr. Franklin succumbed immediately after takeoff, if not before." Dick smiled and continued into the helmet's intercom. "Then I noticed Mr. Fuller twitching and trying to get comfortable, after that Mrs. Franklin watched her husband for a while before scooting over onto her back like she is now." At that Douglas threw a gaze her way as Dick wrapped up his report with "But this other young lady, she only just now passed out. Too scared to let go I guess."

"Yeah, well as scared as I am to let go and hand you the controls I am more than ready to join them, so let's cut the chatter until contact with Sub Base Two, roger that?"

"Roger that." And Dick flew the chopper with its six passengers, four of whom were asleep, no make that five, through the black abyss above that was lit by stars and over a glistening image of it far below.

The hours passed tediously for Dick, whose thoughts kept returning to his own wife still thousands of miles away. Was he putting her through the same torment that this Franklin guy had done to his wife? The thought was conceivable, after all. Peg was strong, strong enough to hide her fears away for his sake, but he knew she would have him home if she could. And Dick remembered how Commander Westfield had rolled his eyes at him when he had told him six months ago that he would marry. "If you really believed in marriage, Dick, you would not do this. This life we have chosen, you and I, is not a nurturing one." And since that moment Dick had asked himself a thousand times if he had done the right thing, but every time a mission was completed and he had a few days to be with Peg, there was never anything more right.

Dick checked his watch before studying the radar, nothing yet. No wait, there's my blip. And he radioed Sub Base Two that they were nearing the rendezvous point.

The activity roused Douglas Westfield into action, sitting up he rubbed his face and took control of the aircraft. He snatched up the 'mic.' and radioed the hidden sub upon seeing the refueling platform lights rising from the sea. "Thanks for being here boys, you are appreciated! We are dropping out of the sky on fumes and extending our hose coupling." He said as the chopper set down and automatic steel rings held it fast to the swaying platform. "Dick, wake our passengers for a break and breakfast, they may have twenty *five* minutes this time!" He grinned.

"Aye, sir!" Was all Commander Westfield heard in reply, and why should there be anything more? They were two soldiers on a mission and did not need to be sociable with each other. Still, sometimes Douglas felt something was missing in his own life. He had not thought of it in a long time, not since Dick's wedding in fact. But this particular mission was not of an ordinary vein and had brought some things to surface. He laughed inwardly at the coincidence of the analogy as their tiny home rocked with the ocean.

When was the last time he'd had a date, or cared to? The only chance he had lately to even think of such a thing was, well, as he was testing Grant Franklin with his own wife. Either the man does not care about her, which does not add up at all, or he really does have amnesia, an admitted possibility after seeing the bump on the man's head for himself. Or he is faking the whole darn thing in order to cover up an extra marital affair, or to hide something else, a something dangerous enough to warrant everyone in his party to keep their mouths shut. Even she would have to stay away from him in order to pull it off! And Douglas studied Jessa as Dick was helping her down from the strap hammock. As he watched her he could not help but notice how longingly she gazed at her husband before dropping her eyes to the floor, and how her reaction made Grant's arms stiffen and his hands form into fists held tightly to his sides as if they were at odds with each other. "Ah, ha, so that's how it is." Douglas rose up from his seat to nonchalantly stretch his limbs before bringing out the rations.

With six people now milling about inside a small area there was little room for standing and yet that was what each one wanted most to do, to stand and stretch and look outside. Grant took his ration of energy bar, water bottle and gum and headed forward for a look about him.

"Just don't touch anything, Mr. Franklin." Westfield warned him as they swayed along with the roll of the ocean. "If you accidentally release our docking rings we will be swept under, and at least one of us will be drowned. I think you know which one." And again Commander Westfield winked at Grant, causing his neck hair to tingle.

After his warning to Grant the others seemed unlikely to explore further than the side door in order to get a view of the ocean. Again the submarine beneath them was not visible, due partly to it being the middle of the night as before, and because it also was painted black like the helicopter-hotel they rode in.

Grant stood alone in the front, using Dick's co pilot seat to lean on and steady himself against the constant rocking of the swells. Appearing to take great notice of the ocean before him, for his face was focused thusly, but from behind no one could tell that his eyes were scanning the massive control panel beneath his supposed field of view. Then his eyes spied what they had been searching for, a small television screen.

It had been turned off as they landed on the platform,

he supposed. He had spotted a tiny camera lens poking out between the computer mouse and the wall shortly after coming on board, and since he did not dare to make any gestures to his wife after seeing it, he promptly pretended to fall asleep, although he knew he had not pretended for long. What had they seen? Had his two friends betrayed their shared secret in some way? What of Jessa? Oh Jessa if only I could explain it all to you now and end this torture. Grant blinked back the tears as he now truly did watch the sea, and it was well that he did, for silently Commander Westfield came up from behind him. Grant took a long drink of the bottled water he had been holding and felt a looming presence too close for comfort.

"Remembering something, Mr. Franklin? About the ocean maybe?"

"That it is on the wrong side, I think. From my home I mean. I guess that's it." Grant told him simply for something to tell the man whom he suspected would pick his brain apart with a tweezers if he could.

"Right." Westfield barely hid his disgust. "Anything else?" And he noticed Jessa and Ian were intently watching their exchange while Dick was showing Mai-Ling the intricacies of the onboard commode. Dick tapped Jessa for guard duty and Mai-Ling handed over her lab coat to be used as a privacy curtain.

Frowning, Grant looked up to meet Westfield's piercing gaze. "No."

Sighing heavily, Douglas took a bite of his ration and chewed. He questioned Ian. "So, you have known Mr. Franklin for a long time, haven't you?"

"About six years." Ian quipped, determined not to give more information than was necessary, yet equally determined not to lie.

Westfield continued. "I find it curious that he remembers what to do with a severed artery, and what side the ocean should be on from his own house, and yet he does not remember his beautiful young wife whose very world rocks to his vibration, so to speak. Mr. Franklin you don't know the half of what this woman has gone through to find you. Allow me to elaborate. After spending what must have seemed like an <u>age</u> of loneliness and fitful nightmares according to Mr. Fuller here, oh yes Ian I remember what you said, she acquired the help of this knight in shining armor here to help her drive through a <u>raging</u> snow storm, the worst in three decades I hear," and he feigned incredulity (at that Jessa and Ian looked at each other in surprise that the Commander knew about their predicament with the storm).

With a flush Mai-Ling emerged from behind the makeshift curtain to exchange places with Jessa. Now she stood guard for the wife of the man she herself proclaimed to be engaged to.

Westfield scrutinized their exchange before turning back to Grant. "After two different hotel stays together," and he paused for effect, for he would say anything if it would make Grant lose his demeanor of witlessness. Humph, nothing. Douglas charged onward with "she showed little hesitation regarding her own safety in coming away with two strange men having vague information about you. Mr. Franklin, your wife took to a canoe in a flooded river at midnight in a communist country that jails Christians for sharing their faith! She <u>generously</u> shared a tiny bottle of air with <u>this</u> dirty old man of a soldier while holding onto the scruff of my neck in a culvert of fast moving flood water and debris, hauled her shivering scrawny body up onto a muddy embankment to hide in the bushes in the cold dark night until what <u>would</u> be enemy soldiers if they had spotted us, left. After all of that, she finds the man of her dreams kissing another woman! <u>This</u> woman that is holding up her lab coat so that she can relieve herself!" And there was another flush as Jessa emerged from behind the white coat. "Gentlemen, would any of <u>you</u> have believed such a cock and bull story? Do <u>I</u> look stupid to you Mr. Franklin?" The commander seemed genuinely interested to know.

Dick was getting an unusual debriefing to be sure. "Doug seems pretty worked up over something." He thought as he dumped some chemical into the bowl to dissolve the waste.

Grant braced himself for a blow as he coldly refused to

buckle to temptation. There was too much at stake and only he knew exactly how much. "Look, mister." He spoke up. "I am glad you will have a story to tell your grandchildren when you finally retire from this man's army, and I am grateful to you for bringing me back to my own country, along with these good people that apparently I care very much about, if I could only remember, but I don't! Someday maybe I will. Maybe something or someone will trigger everything to return, but I don't <u>know</u>!"

"Sub Base Two to Air Base One. Your tank is full, have a safe flight home Commander!" The radio filled the room and stirred movement from every single person, who for a brief moment had been intensely still. Grabbing the 'mic.' now, Commander Westfield thanked them and ordered a "Return to Land Base." Then he ordered the people in the chopper to return to their positions for flight, and within sixty seconds flat they had scrambled to seats and hammocks, and Dick reported, "All secure." A pre-flight check, rings released, and upward like a shot they catapulted.

Again Jessa could hear next to her Mai-Ling gasping as they felt the push against gravity in their swinging cages. In a minute they leveled off once more and continued their race to meet sunrise, which proved to be unlike any they had known, for being above the curvature of the earth and far from any mountain, with only ocean all around there was nothing to slow or to block the rays of the vibrant orb. An orange hue rose to the horizon then instantly the brightness of it burst into and filled every bit of space in the helicopter. The pilots activated a sunshield and the room became tinted in dark green, like a jungle in twilight.

The roar of the mighty helicopter would drown out any words spoken by the four in back, but Jessa looked down at her husband anyway to mouth the words "I love you."

An ever so faint smile played at Grant's lips as he closed his eyes in pretended sleep.

Sighing heavily, Jessa rolled over onto her back to do the same, and Mai-Ling followed her example. Ian frowned a bit as he looked over at the pilots, and then closed his eyes to the world.

They had re-crossed the international dateline now, and had a day to live over. Although it seemed very much like the one before, being stuck in a machine flying high above the earth and unable to communicate or even to move about, yet this day shone brightly with hope for Jessa.

CHAPTER TWENTYFIVE

A SOLDIER'S GENEROSITY

It had been months since Mai- Ling had seen sunshine, yet now as she was flown over American shoreline and thrown into a new life it shone like a beacon to all who would be free. There above the clouds of white and gray below, all was azure sky. Though the sunshield dimmed its brightness, the warm rays assured her that all would be well and for the first time since the landslide had claimed her father, a small smile tugged at her mouth as her spirit was gracefully lifted from a heavy depression.

"At least my father's wish is fulfilled." She thought. "That I may live in a land of choice. I may choose to become a Christian, I can live where I wish, work at any kind of job and marry a man I choose." She happened to gaze downward now in her reverie and her eyes found Ian lying below. He was still sleeping. She remembered in the hospital ward how he had called Grant by some other name, Kent, was it? She did not know then or now why, but it was something so deep it had stopped a fight. She was certain Mr. Franklin would not have won if that Westfield man had not intervened. Still, this one named Ian had come all this way to help his friend, he must be a very special kind of person to honor them so, but it was curious how he did not seem pleased with the outcome. "He is very handsome," she decided "for a westerner. I am glad Mr. Westfield did not have to hurt him. If my Tai had come sooner they both would have been in a heap." She missed her cousin.

In that moment Ian awoke to find a pretty round face with

black almond shaped eyes cast upon him. The eyes popped open wide which caused her cheeks to blush and the pretty face spun away. He smiled broadly, thinking she was too young for him anyway. He looked around the room, particularly at the pilots. He could see only the backsides of their helmets and yet Commander Westfield boomed out "Good morning, Mr. Fuller! Welcome to the good old U.S. of A.! Land of the free, home of the brave! We are currently passing over Idaho and are soon to set down on the Bozeman airstrip and heli-base."

"How did he know I was awake?" Ian shook his head in wonder as he pulled the lever to sit the chair uprightly. He smiled up at Jessa who was now stretching and yawning above him.

She felt elated! Smiling brightly up at the ceiling she thought of the happy days to come. If they could only get away from these government men, she and Grant could return to their wilderness home and maybe even start a family, for what could be better than that?

But when Commander Westfield asked her "And how are you this fine morning, Mrs. Franklin? I trust you slept well?"

She sobered her face to look his way from her hanging basket of a cage to yell back her response "I'm fine, thank you Mr. Westfield!"

The cabin monitor's small screen was not at the high level of the hammocks and so he had not been able to watch her face, only those of the men below. He was hoping for more than that polite bit. "Of course it may be because it is so hard to hear right now." He mused.

They had blasted through the imaginary border of rugged terrain far below and into Montana's airspace when Commander Westfield dropped their altitude and slowed the chopper's speed to an almost ordinary flight approach to the Bozeman airport.

"Time out, twelve minutes remaining." Dick reported to his commander.

"Alright, well done soldier." Doug commended his junior officer over their intercom. Then thoughtfully added, "You have ten days shore leave coming and I want you to go spend it with that pretty wife of yours."

Dick's eyebrows raised and a smile yanked his face to show white teeth. "Yes sir! Thank you sir!" He could not remember ever having appreciated anything his commander had said so much as this. Later he would call Peg and inform her to stock the fridge and disconnect the phone because "I'm coming home!" And after, Peg was to present him with prepaid tickets out of Florida on a cruise to the Southern Caribbean, top deck suite, first class all the way, and all a gift from Doug. "He does have his moments." Dick would say kindly of Doug from a private balcony of the speeding ship, overlooking the sea with a tall glass in one hand and Peg's slim waist in a sheer white slip in the other.

Setting down on land now, Dick disconnected from his helmet and shot out of the chopper so fast that Doug could not stifle his laughter, as he watched his young cohort run to the hangar and practically rip the huge door from its hinges, as he laid into it with his shoulder to shove it open on a run.

"Well now, he can be motivated!" Douglas smirked, and at that the commander guided the monster machine ever so carefully into the hangar, past the utility truck that waited for him and up to the Franklin's Suburban, then allowed the mighty chopper's engine to slowly shut down. He released himself from the pilot seat's straps and stood to stretch mightily as the others inside did the same. "Miss Cho" He informed Mai-Ling. "You were whisked away rather abruptly, do you have your passport with you? No? Any identification to show you clear U.S. inspection? No, of course not. Well let's take care of that little detail right now, shall we?" And Douglas went to the computer, flipped on the power, selected a special font and paper type, and began typing. He extracted a digital camera from a drawer to snap a picture of Mai-Ling in her soiled and rumpled lab coat and mussed hair. He slipped it into the scanner and in a few moments the printer spat out an official document which he laminated and placed into a small rectangular blue folding pouch. "And 'wala' he announced, seemingly pleased with himself. "You keep this with you at all times and you will not have any trouble, guaranteed."

"This is officiaw?" Mai-Ling inquired incredulously while hoping she was not offending, but it was all so much a surprise. Not realizing it she began rocking back and forth, her habit when extremely excited.

At his smiling response "Better than official, miss Cho." She shed a tear and thanked him profusely while bowing several times. Years later she would look at the picture and inwardly wish that she had removed the dirty lab coat and smoothed her hair before allowing the picture to be taken. But she was official. She had the right to be free!

Dick stood in the open door of the chopper. Leaning in he smiled at the exchange between Mai-Ling and his commander. "Everyone ready to move out? Mr. Fuller, toss me your luggage and I will run it over to the Suburban." Dick smiled giddily. Ian did so and as he spun around for Jessa's duffle bag he noticed that Dick was being literal, for he ran with Ian's three pieces of luggage, which of course had proven to be simply along for the ride.

Ian felt something, although he was not at all sure what, for this Westfield guy. Like finishing a good book and wishing there were more, even if you did not like all of the characters in it they are essential to the adventure. He held out his hand to grasp that of the Commander. "God's speed, sir."

"Well, what do you know?" And Doug gave him a half smile as he shook Ian's hand in earnest. He genuinely liked this man who had done so much for a friend, even if the guy did not like to fly.

Jessa handed Ian the keys as he helped Mai-Ling out of the chopper and they walked across the space to the Flyer.

Douglas addressed Jessa now with "Ma'am, I hope this punk scientist is everything you ever dreamed of, you certainly deserve him to be. You will forgive me if I have my doubts?" And at her sheepish smile he added, "What I said back at the hospital still stands. If he does not stack up I will know. And we will be seeing each other again, that is money in the bank."

Again Jessa offered him her hand, and this time and much to her relief, he merely shook it. "Thank you for everything. What is your favorite meal?" She inquired. "Since we will be seeing you again, I mean." And she, still having his hand, used it to pull herself in close for a hug. "I appreciate you, and what you do. And I look forward to visiting with you. But later, please? I need to be with Grant, alone for a while at least, catching up and figuring out what we can do for him. I am sure you have a legion of psychologists you can call upon, but let me try first, please?" And at her urgent pleading he caved, only a bit, but his plans to whisk Grant away to a D.C. compound melted. After all, there were other ways to get what he wanted, one of which was already set into place.

Westfield grimaced and shook his head at her but said "Alright, you have it your way for now. I will be checking in on him, though. He may have information I need, and if you appreciate what I do, you can appreciate my quest for knowledge." At that Douglas stepped back, lifted Jessa's hand to his mouth and kissed the back of it goodbye, then turned to her husband.

"Mr. Franklin you need to remember this young lady in order to receive the greatest blessings any man can have. I expect that when you do, other memories will naturally fall into place. Here is my card. If you find things returning to your head about your work as a geologist, this great country will appreciate your returning to work." And at that, Douglas waved them out to follow their friends to the Flyer.

Ian had opened the front door for Mai-Ling and he had the vehicle's engine warming when Grant and Jessa scrambled into the middle seat.

Waving their goodbyes as Ian drove them out into the sunlight and heading toward Jessa's parents' home, all were incredibly relieved at their being let go without having to fight for Grant's freedom, or being detained in some sort of government complex.

"I can't believe it!" Jessa piped excitedly, to which Grant held a bony finger to his chapped lips for all to see. Reaching into his soiled lab jacket pocket, he pulled out the card Commander Westfield had given him. Holding it up for all to see, he pointed to the backside and motioned to his ears. The card was a listening device. Then silently Grant leaned forward to reach into Mai-Ling's coat pocket and extract the gift of her new passport. Pointing to it and again to his ears, his finger went back to his lips as he rolled both the cards up in his lab coat and motioned for Mai-Ling to lock them into the glove compartment.

Ian had been watching things from his peripheral vision as he spoke up for all to hear "So shall we head to your folks' home, Jessa?" And he turned on the radio.

"Yes, let's do that, Ian. And let's all go out to breakfast, shall we? After we clean up, of course." They chatted all the way to her mom and dad's home about many things, but nothing was said about unusual weather, earthquakes or love, or plans for the future beyond the immediate.

Pulling into the James' driveway now, Ian parked and shut off the engine. Exiting the vehicle Jessa heard the sounds of chatting in the back yard, and rounding the side of the house she was nearly knocked down by a hurtling hairy mass of excitement that had effortlessly jumped the gate. "Bozeman!" She cried happily while laughing and hugging her dog. Then he stiffened at the new arrivals, took notice of Mai-Ling looking at him all wide-eyed while smelling her fear, then stared at the hairy image of his master. He was skinny and tired, unshaven and yet, smiling down at him. "Woof!" Bozeman jumped forward to paw Grant for his attention and affection.

"Hey, old man." Grant squatted to pet his dog. "I hear you have been doing a fine job protecting Jessa, thank you!" Grant spoke softly as he was still not sure of being free from observation. He was not sure of revealing anything yet.

"Why it's Grant he's after! Bozeman, save a piece for me!" And Yvonne came out to hug her son in law. Making his decision, Grant stood slowly with arms limp at his side, as he asked "Bozeman who?"

Yvonne's head popped up off of Grant's shoulder as if she

thought she had been accidentally hugging a stranger. Looking worried she informed him "Grant, I am your mother in law, Mrs. James! We've known each other for years! You bought this dog from me for Jessa, your wife." And she swung a hand toward her daughter for emphasis.

Swallowing hard, Grant responded. "Well thank you, Mrs. James. I will file the information away and maybe it will help to jar my memory. And is this your husband?"

Jessa's dad shook the hand of his wayward in law, and then excused himself to the bathroom, shaking his head all the while.

"Mom could we all go inside?" Jessa asked tensely and motioned for everyone to proceed to the front door.

Once inside Grant queried quietly "Mrs. James, has there been anyone unusual in your home lately? I mean like a cable company, gas or electric worker? No? Are you <u>sure</u>?" He persisted as he looked around and felt under the table, and then pulled out a chair to climb on and peer into the light shade hanging from the ceiling.

"Let's ask dad." Alice said as her husband emerged from the bathroom. "Wes, has anyone been in the house besides our family lately?"

Frowning up at Grant until his son in law was satisfied that there was no 'bug' hiding in their light fixture, and so stepped down from the dining room chair, Wes answered his wife "No, not that I know of but you know we haven't always been here, either."

The thought occurred to Jessa "What about Debra? Maybe she let someone in while you were out?"

"Oh no dear, we always locked our door and she never wanted to see anybody anyway. She stayed in her room all alone, just her and her misery."

"Past tense, mom? Isn't she here?" Jessa was surprised.

Dad answered his daughter this time. "She packed up and lit out of here for Texas, to chase after Tom! This is the first time she has shown enough gumption to make any effort to win a man back!" And dad smiled a laugh.

"Yes, maybe it will all work out after all!" Mom hoped aloud. "It was after you left with your friend here that she asked us to have bible study with her, the first time in years. We weren't ready then to be much help to her, but now we can be. I didn't know she even had the good book, but we opened it together and she seemed to perk up a bit. She got herself into a cold shower and changed her smelly clothes, cleaned up very nicely if you ask me, didn't she dad?"

"Yeah." Was all Jessa's misty-eyed father could muster by this point.

"And Jessa," Mom volunteered "this time she took the good book with her." Mom smiled and reached out for dad's hand.

Feeling a rush of hope within her for her sister, Jessa joined her parents in a group hug. Inviting everyone to join them, a group of six believers prayed for the one who sought happiness on the open road to Texas, and for their own safety.

Mai-Ling had never been privy to such an open and honest bequest on the behalf of another, and wished she could write to her cousin about it, but knew the letter would be studied and destroyed by the mail censors the day it arrived in China.

"Jessa honey, now that we have been in close quarters with all of you, well, would you all like to take showers and change into fresh clothing? I don't know how else to say it, please forgive me." And Yvonne snickered her embarrassment while Wesley laughed out loud.

Everyone laughed at least a little and Ian excused himself to retrieve his suitcase and Jessa's duffle bag, which he carried up the stairs for her.

Jessa and Mai-Ling climbed the stairs to the upper bathroom that was smaller yet more private. Ian and Grant took turns showering and shaving on the ground floor and Mr. James loaned Grant a pair of slacks and a dress shirt. Mrs. James brought clothes for Mai-Ling from Debra's room and excused herself to return to her kitchen to create brunch for six.

Now in her element, Yvonne cooked an assortment of hash browned potatoes, vegetable omelets and French toast, while Wesley mixed the orange juice and set the table.

Ian could hear the two of them chatting in the kitchen as they went about their tasks, and inwardly wondered if he would ever have that kind of relationship. The possibilities seemed miniscule, in fact he could not see any at all, not anymore. The bit of conversation between himself and Grant in the bathroom was strained at best. Neither man was sure of their own relationship as friends at the moment. Each had issues with the other that could not be conveniently broached at the moment, if ever.

Ian emerged first with clean black jeans and black and emerald plaid shirt, and had left his smelly cowboy's boots outside to don his shining black dress shoes instead. His shaggy, thick, black wavy hair clung moistly to his head, his chiseled features now freshly shaven of stubble and his teeth shone. He would have smiled more perhaps if they had found Grant dead, he guiltily admitted to himself. But it <u>was</u> good to see his friend alive, if not so well, even though he knew that the memory loss was a ruse and that soon enough Grant and Jessa could drop the foolery and move on together. He remembered his promise to himself that no matter what, he would see this thing through for Jessa's sake, and now that test was upon him. He <u>must</u> let go his dream of her.

Ian turned to look up the stairs when he heard the door open, and a feeling of 'déjà vu' swept over him, for once again he saw two lovely ladies descending a staircase toward him. One he recognized in her flowered blue cotton dress with the white lace overlay, though instead of boots Jessa sported her new high heeled strap sandals. He understood; she would keep the red velvet dress for private dinners with Grant, and something hurt inside himself.

But this other young woman, who had suddenly become more than a mere girl, was a pleasant surprise. No more rumpled lab coat with mussed hair, no more the frantic lost look. Mai-Ling wore the only type of skirt that Debra had left behind, a brown leather mini that was not too awfully short on Mai, as Ian would come to call her. Her feet <u>almost</u> filled the black pointed toe, pump shoes that held delicately curving calves. Her tiny waist let the skirt slip and slide, this way and that, as she moved gracefully along. Her red lips parted ever so slightly when she met his gaze. He noticed a change in her breathing just then as the sheer, long sleeved white blouse with ruffles down the middle stopped its intriguing motion. Jessa stopped short on the last step and motioned for Mai-Ling to continue. Ian had not planned any such thing, but years of programming kicked in and he offered his arm to Mai. She hesitated for a moment then smiled shyly and accepted.

Jessa watched the two acquaintances, and something hurt inside her, but she put it away as she waited with butterflies in her stomach for the rest room door to open, and as it did so she went to him, pushing him gently back inside then closing and locking the door behind her. Turning to her husband they clung together in wordless embrace, allowing the tears to flow freely.

Grant could hold it in no longer. "Jessa, my Jessa! Please forgive me; please, please, please can you forgive me? There was no other way! They are watching me, listening everywhere. I can't tell where I'm safe. Please love me! Say you love me, please. I love you so much!"

"Grant, I do love you! I've never stopped loving you! This moment is an answer to prayer! Oh God, my God thank You! I was so afraid I would never see you again my darling! And now..." And she could not continue.

"My darling I will <u>never</u> leave you again! I moved the funding to our account to use from home. Things will be very different from now on! We will have electricity, and hot running water and a real road into town! And a family, Jessica! If you can see being mother to the offspring of an intellectually challenged moron like me! Please say yes, but only if it is still what <u>you</u> want?"

Jessa tried to speak but without Grant to hold her up she would have hyperventilated to the floor.

He picked her up in his arms and held her close. "Breathe slowly sweetheart, slowly in, slowly out. There's my girl, in, now out. Feel a little better now?" And she nodded her head slowly as she smiled at him through tears of utter joy.

"I understand now. For the first time I truly understand the story of the prodigal son; a heart broken father, who waited and watched for his wayward son to return, and the incredible joy when he did come home because he was not lost anymore. Yes, Grant, yes please!" And she put her face against his and kissed him over and over again.

Everyone in the kitchen had fortunately been hungry enough to proceed with their meal in spite of the muffled conversation emanating from the bathroom, for Yvonne could not abide allowing her efforts to get cold, and they enjoyed a scrumptious breakfast.

Thirty minutes had passed before the lock on the bathroom door could be heard opening. Slowly the door opened and Grant peered out. He smiled sheepishly before stepping out, his hand holding Jessa's, which he tucked under his arm. She was beaming beautifully, her tears having been wiped away by Grant's loving hand.

The couple stood before their family and friends and Grant announced to all "I remember now. I am married to Jessa and nothing else matters!"

"Oh, that's wonderful!" Yvonne cried, and kissed her son in law's freshly shaven cheek. "And you are so much more handsome without those long whiskers!" She laughed and employed them to "Please sit down, you both are so skinny these days, eat some food!"

CHAPTER TWENTYSIX

GOODBYE, BOZEMAN

Twelve days had passed since Grant had said goodbye to his parents. They came home today and everyone celebrated at a party hosted by Grant and Jessa. The festivities were held outside in the couple's roofed and flowering garden, which Jorge` had kept beautifully colorful and pruned.

"Thank you, everyone!" Grant's father addressed the crowd of well- wishers. "For joining us in our joy today, for our son who was lost is now found and back among us!" A smiling Don lifted his glass of sparkling cider in a toast to Grant and Jessa. The couple seemed never to stop holding hands.

Ian flew home after calling his parents, and accompanied by a less than assured Mai- Ling, the two had left the country she had dreamed of for so many years, to fly to Canada and prepare another welcome for their friends, a welcome home.

Grant had removed the electronic wire from Mai's passport before handing it over to her, and along with the card that Westfield had given him, stored them both in a safe deposit box in town.

Grant and Jessa enjoyed a second honeymoon of sorts before his parents had returned from their mission work. And now they said their goodbyes once again with the promise of soon having a guest room built on to their cabin.

The Franklins took their time driving back home, stopping to see the sights along the way, for it was their own company that was now the most important thing in the world, and the days were filled with sharing and giving.

Bozeman enjoyed having both his master and mistress together again, and like a child at play he would bring them treasures he found along the way, sticks to throw and retrieve, a deflated rubber ball, Frisbee, a smashed toy car. Useless items, really, but in their heightened state of joy even the humans seemed to relish every bit of trifle their 'child' uncovered.

"Oooh, nice rock, Bozie!" Jessa would squeal and pat her panting dog, or "Great Scott! Look what the Bozester has found, darling!" from Grant. It had been all too long since he'd had the attention of both, and so happily the great canine would dash off to rummage through another park bush, snatch up another find and gallop back to them. The air was cold and their breath flew out of their mouths in a fine misty exhaust as they spoke, though they had not felt this warm hearted in ages.

It took four days of meandering northward, for the couple was in no hurry as in times past to leave or to return to their tiny valley home. All that mattered was that they were together and whenever Bozeman showed signs of weariness they would load up and travel on. What child would not feel special to have their whimsy satisfied thusly?

Upon arriving at last back at Fuller Lodge, the Franklins were greeted with fanfare and balloons, songs and dancing, dinner and dessert, and a night 'On the house' in the ranch's honeymoon cottage.

Mai-Ling had been offered a job as Irene's understudy, which she gratefully accepted, saying, "It is good to be useful and to have purpose." The young woman smiled broadly, bowing her head all the while, grateful to be accepted into their little community. Mai-Ling was surprised at how the people she met at the ranch were accepting of her, even though there were none around who looked like her. Mai stuck to Irene like glue, learning in detail the many tasks to perform that made Fuller Lodge run smoothly. She was given a small room next to Irene's in the basement. She took her meals after waiting tables and serving in the restaurant, and it soon became apparent to Evelyn that her son would wait to eat until Mai-Ling had cleared the tables and headed to the kitchen to have a meal, where he would coincidentally meet her there and sup with her.

"I'm just helping her to adjust, mom. She has no friends except the Franklins and myself, that are her age, I mean. Okay, so I <u>am</u> older." A long pause as Ian stared into his steaming cup that morning. "Mom, do you think I am <u>too</u> old for her?" And biting his lower lip Ian looked slowly up into his mother's eyes, the question staring up at her from her beloved son's face, asking, "Could Mai be the one?"

Evelyn's smile was infectious. "Ian, I asked Mai-Ling her age before offering her this job. I was concerned she might not be old enough to work the banquet bar. She is twenty-four years old, dear. Old enough?"

Ian launched from his chair, kissed his mother and went to seek out Irene's understudy.

Evelyn heard the lobby door open and close in the foyer and she stepped lightly around the corner of the white walled kitchen to find Grant and Jessa, holding hands as always, smiling and about to ring the bell.

"Good morning, Mr. Franklin! Mrs. Franklin. Did you sleep well?"

"Never better!" Jessa appreciated Evelyn's query.

"Mrs. Fuller?" Grant asked of Evelyn "Could you and Josef join us after breakfast to discuss a land right of way proposal? We will pay for all the work done on a paved single lane road from our cabin to the lodge, and continue it on and into town. I believe you and your customers would enjoy it very much?" He smiled broadly. "And it would be a great relief to us when the time for starting our family arrives." Grant lovingly kissed Jessa's lips.

Evelyn was thrilled at the concept and left them to call her husband, who was shoeing a couple of horses in the stable.

The two lovebirds breakfasted with hot plates of pancakes and scrambled eggs, biscuits with brown gravy and orange juice and orange slices. Then they got to work.

Grant and Jessa met with the Fullers, all but Lorene who had returned to Alaska until Christmas. Grant offered to let the ranch hands do the work of clearing the trees and excavating the road in preparation for paving, which would be a sure moneymaker for the ranch. With the use of their logging equipment this was accomplished and a paving company brought in to pour and flatten the road.

All the while that the road was being built, a basement was dug and phone and power lines added. A guest room and two more bedrooms were added, and a septic tank!

Grant had also acquired a few specialty items. His own high- powered computer, satellite dish receiver complete with remote control, a palmtop with holographic keyboard for travel, and not last nor least, an electronics sniffing, handheld robot. Never again would he have to worry about who may be listening. He would stay home with Jessa, and he would continue his work. He would train others in earthquake detection via electronic classes that he would teach with the help of his live cam computer screen.

All of which was done from the basement, which could only be accessed by the remote controlled floor that slid aside and revealed steps to Grant's laboratory, as he so giddily referred to it.

And when the visit came, Jessa made Commander Douglas Westfield feel at home, with the best chicken cordon bleu he had ever had "This side of the continent!" He declared.

Grant was able to maintain that he taught classes from home and he would not take any other job. Jessa's bulging tummy and healthy glow convinced the Commander she had what she wanted, and when he kissed her hand for the last time as he left, he reached out for Grant's hand to shake, and was pleasantly surprised to receive it. "Well done, Mr. Franklin. America and this whole world are looking forward to your apprentices going to work! Thank you sir and good luck." And with that Douglas left in his rented S.U.V. for the airport to fly back to Washington D.C.

Grant closed the cabin door as Jessa handed him 'Sniffy', which he used to scan the house as they kept up a monologue. "Well that was a nice visit, don't you think, dear?" Jessa said as she started the dishwasher.

"Mmm, hmm." Her husband waved the device slowly around the room and under the dining table. "Blip- blip!" And Grant knelt to look underneath the hardwood top to extract a 'bug'. He picked up a lead box from atop the new hearth. "Do you think Mr. Westfield is losing his hair?" Grant grinned as he deposited the electronic creature. Another "Blip." And he moved to the chair their company had sat on.

"Oh, you may be right about that. Putting on weight, too I believe." Jessa silently snickered as her husband plunked a second device into the box. Waving about the house again Grant found three more 'bugs' before being satisfied that the area was clean. Then he went outside, took one from the front door, one from above the woodpile and another from a windowsill. "Oh, you sneaky dog!" Grant reproved as he shook his box of 'bugs' and laughed.

Pulling a book from the shelf above the piano, Grant pulled the lever down and the floor slid back to present shiny metal steps dropping to a soundproof room that was filled with its own electronic toys. Extending his hand to her, Grant led Jessa to their lab. "I need to show you something sweetheart." And his fingers flew over the computer's keyboard. A graph appeared and began filling in a map of their area, a geographical map that alongside of which were dates and magnitudes of past earthquakes. Ridges and valleys, plains and mountains, all had some statistical data of tremors and jolts, all except their tiny valley. "This is why I chose this speck of ground. These seventy-five acres of undisturbed soil, that has never known an earthquake and shows no sign of ever going to. Do you have any idea of how unusual that is? How very rare even? I have begun a new study, a statistical study so far, that may give more clues as to how earthquakes travel throughout our world, like a huge worm. Now here are data of centuries past, giving some inkling of how at times, coincidences of quakes striking on one side of the globe were followed up on the other side. Here are data of more recent quakes, emanating from China's centralized mining operations. The dates and times correlate with distance traveled to other countries. Distance through the earth at quake speed that is."

"Grant, what are you saying?" Jessa's neck hair felt strange.

He looked up from the computer screen to meet her worried gaze. "I believe that the Chinese government has found a way to utilize their hundreds of miles of old mining tunnels to create, and <u>send</u> quaking jolts to other countries. And I believe one of these countries was Taiwan, which China has been after for years to bring back under their original government.

Silence.

"Grant, has anyone else seen this?"

"No. And I am not sure what I can do about it."

"But why didn't you tell Commander Westfield?"

"Because my love, he has been battling it out with that country with his own super weapon, weather manipulation."

Jessa gasped. "What? Can you be serious? Grant, this is all so very…"

"Hard to take, I know. But look." And his fingers took flight once more to bring up satellite data. "These satellites are American. These are not. Now look at their different rotations and orbit patterns. Only the American brand does this." And he brought up the change in orbit that the U.S. satellites displayed at certain points in their flight over the earth. They dipped closer to the earth at times, whereas the satellites of other countries did not. And the computer showed a smooth plunge on graph lines, then came up again to follow the predisposed flight path. He stood from his chair to grab a fold of graph paper to show his wife. "And I had noticed this on the mountain, before the landslide." Grant winced at the memory. "My probe's readouts had shown me this before, but <u>only</u> when I used American satellites! And there is this, (he pointed to the overlaying wiggling lines on the graph) a type of vibration, not a naturally occurring phenomenon but an <u>artificial</u> atmospheric disturbance! And the only thing I have ever seen that even comes close to having that kind of sophistication would be the helicopter we flew home in! Jessa, these satellites are dipping precisely over China, or rather, they were, and for precisely long enough to cross that country! <u>That</u> country that loses hundreds of miners yearly to accidents that could be avoided under normal operations. And that country that has seasonal flooding so severe as to have lost seventeen thousand of its people, including Mai-Ling Cho's mother and three siblings."

Jessa gasped, and Grant continued. "Her cousin was raised as a brother to her because he is the only flood survivor in his family."

Grant proceeded to show Jessa other evidences of weather manipulation. He showed her how the fires in Oregon and California had scorched a half million acres then suddenly been doused by a freakish August storm, some called it an Inland hurricane, or Microburst.

"And sweetheart, this is why Douglas Westfield has been so very interested in us. He believes I know."

A shock of fear ran up Jessa's spine. "What would he do?"

"I don't know. Lock us away perhaps. But don't be afraid my love, for don't you see? All of this, these wars and rumors of wars, earthquakes in different places than they have ever been, freakish and unpredictable weather, is only prophecy fulfilling itself!" He beamed.

Jessa smiled at his reassurance. "I know. And when I hear of a river running backward I will know our Lord is nearly here to take us home, to heaven." And Jessa hugged her husband.

They climbed the stairs arm in arm, replaced the flooring and retired for the night.

In the morning blast of cold air that heralds the winter morning they awoke and dressed in their new attire for a very special day, a wedding. Bozeman was let into the back and they drove away in the Flyer to the ranch.

It would be an indoor affair as the weather was frightfully cold and the snow, which had come weeks before, remained frozen to the ground. Upon entering the lodge they were greeted by Ian and Lorene who were accepting gifts and charging each guest to sign the Guest book. Jessa signed them in while Grant handed over a large gift, and hand in hand they proceeded to the fireplace in the restaurant, and chatted with Karen who had come to play for the happy event. The large room was nearly full when Ian announced it was time to begin, for everyone had arrived. He remained standing at the foot of the stairs and nodded to Karen.

Karen began the Wedding March and all looked expectantly to the staircase. Stepping ever so lightly down the steps came a beautifully clad Mai-Ling in a peach satin kimono, with her hair up and tiny peach blossoms pinned into her bun. Holding a bouquet of Bird of Paradise and Baby's Breath, her pink satin slippers touched the last step. Mai-Ling and Ian bowed to each other and she went on through the restaurant foyer, passing by the appreciative crowd, and to the dance floor to stand opposite of 'Doc', her slender form shimmering in the candle light.

Next came Irene in a mid length, pale pink satin dress with a short waist jacket. Her hair was coiffed under a small, matching satin cap with short white veil over her face. Her hands gloved in white held a cascading bouquet of white rose buds and green fern.

When Irene's silk pumps touched the floor, she took Ian's offered arm and together they walked past the crowd of friends, past the warm fire, on by Karen at the piano and to the awaiting groom.

'Doc' wore a prideful air. He could hardly believe this was happening to him! "Why, if it had not been for Dody, I would die a lonely old man!" He thought and smiled broadly at his dear old friend in the crowd who waved her tissue at him, then back to his bride. "How beautiful she is! Why didn't I think of this before?" Harris breathed under his breath.

The music stopped as Ian kissed Irene's cheek, then placed her hand into 'Doc's and Irene handed over her bouquet to Mai-Ling to hold so that she and Harris could walk unencumbered to the minister.

After they were pronounced man and wife, Irene and Harris made their rounds hand in hand, chatting with their friends and family, then leading the way to the brunch buffet, and when they had their fill Harris and Irene danced together for the very first time as husband and wife.

Lorene marched up to Irene at the end of the number and reminded her of a certain tradition.

"Ladies!" Lorene yelled at the top of her lungs. "It is time for the bride to throw the bouquet!" And with squeals of delight all the young (and young at heart) maidens came forth to claim their right to be the next one to be wed.

Smiling joyfully Irene turned away from the eager throng and flung her hefty bouquet up as high and far as she could muster, which landed square on the beam above her. There were groans and peals of laughter at the awkward situation. One ranch hand let out a howl of relief, which earned him a smack of disapproval from his date.

Perplexed, Mai-Ling stood looking up at the flowers dangling from their lofty height. "Why she throw fwowers to ceiwing?" She wanted to know.

Ian composed himself enough to explain that traditionally, the woman to catch the flowers would be the next one to be married.

"Ooh..." And Mai's eyes got big. "They marry!"

Ian looked down to see her intent gaze and realization of the tradition.

Mai had sometime ago wondered why Ian was not married, but would never have been so bold as to ask him.

She drew a conclusion. "Now these women cannot marry because this bouquet is stuck? We can put tables and chairs up and knock it down with a broom so they can marry. I will do this so they can marry, okay?"

And when Mai-Ling moved as if to pull a table under the beam Ian quickly caught hold of her.

"No! No Mai, it's okay. They can marry without having that bouquet. And they will when the time is right. But right now is Irene and 'Doc's time, you see?"

She looked at him and at his hand on her arm, then bowed her head and quietly asked "When is right time for you?" She blushed and looked at the floor.

Ian's breath caught in his throat as he said sullenly, "I don't know. I wish I knew. I thought it was right twice before, but I was wrong."

And when Mai looked up again Ian's face was flushed, and

he released her to stride to the den, leaving her to stand alone in the crowd.

Hours later, after the newlyweds had opened their gifts to the "Oohs" and "Aahs" and howls of laughter, after the confetti had been swept up and tables bussed and dishes washed, after the newlyweds were whisked away to the honeymooner's cottage, and after all the crowd had gone, Mai came back to the restaurant again, this time in her black spandex pedal pusher pants to move a table under the beam that held captive her right to marry. She put up a chair on the table, and a tall bucket upside down on top of that. From the kitchen she extracted the long push broom and proceeded to climb her makeshift tower. On her tiptoes Mai could barely reach the piece of pink satin ribbon that dangled against the beam, but it was enough for the broom to pull the rest down.

A faint knock came at the den door as Ian was slaving over inventory at the computer, anything to keep his mind off of Mai-Ling's question. A little louder it came until he roused and opened the door. "Yes? A bewildered yawn escaped his mouth. Then he quickly sobered as he realized who it was and what she had.

Standing before him holding the beautiful bouquet she had risked life and limb to rescue, a hopeful Mai-Ling asked graciously, "Is it time for you to marry, <u>now</u>?"

CHAPTER TWENTYSEVEN

THE END BEFORE THE BEGINNING (ONE YEAR LATER)

Grant stared at the computer screen, unresponsive. Jessa tried again. "Grant! Are you ready to go?" It seemed a simple enough question. Why didn't he answer? Little Benjamin was cooing and spluttering in his car chair, shaking his plastic keys as his mother looked adoringly at him, then back downstairs to her husband. Had he suddenly gone deaf? What was he looking at anyway?

He remembered hearing her voice as if at the end of a long tunnel. He stood in the middle of the tunnel between her and eternity. The Hubble telescope was showing him a picture of that eternity. In his mind's eye he fancied he could see it moving toward him.

His wife's gentle hand found his shoulder. "Sweetheart, are you ready to go?" Those profound words echoed in his soul.

"<u>Am</u> I ready to go?" He pondered aloud.

"Yes, that is what I have been asking you. It is nearly the time. What are you looking at? It's beautiful!"

"The constellation Orion, the Birthplace of the Stars. You have seen it on one of our daily devotional books, remember? You said the formation of the stars on the cover looked like a dove. Well here they are, and astronomers believe they are coming closer. He is coming for us at last, Jess! I think I am ready. Or at least I thought I was, but now that time has run out to <u>become</u> ready I feel, squeamish. We live on a planet that has corrupted itself so badly that our LORD will not even step foot on it again until he has cleansed it with fire and made it new when He returns again, after having cleansed His believers for a thousand years in heaven. Then 'woe be it' to those arising into the second resurrection."

Jessa's fixed stare wavered from her husband to the panorama of the computer screen. She felt the need to sit down and found her husband's lap. "How soon? Can you tell?" She buried her face in his.

"No. And as the bible states, "No man can know the day nor the hour, but my Father in heaven. But we can know the season."

Jessa gasped.

"Please don't be afraid, my love." Grant comforted.

She smiled "I felt a movement, here." And she put his hand on her tummy. Inside her their daughter was forming. "I am not afraid my love, but relieved."

Together they knelt and prayed for the coming of Jesus, prayed for their family and friends to be ready, and for all who would come into Christianity to do so <u>now</u> in order to be saved for eternity with God.

"Amen."

They both rose up, and climbing the stairs to pick up Benjamin they headed for the 'Flyer', and to Mai and Ian's wedding.

"It is finished."

ABOUT THE AUTHOR

Carolyn Moor

Born in Portland, Oregon in spring of 1959, I long had inkling to do this "Some day", which has finally come at last. Dropping inhibitions has been a necessary task for this once introverted child.

Like Jessa, horses were my first love, before meeting my husband of soon to be twenty- five years. At age eighteen we married, and after a nine- year honeymoon we started a family.

Raising children is the great adventure of my life as the honeymoon continues, every season showing fresh changes and new adventures in living. Volunteering has been a way of life for my husband and I, he a volunteer firefighter of twenty-four years experience in our growing community of Cornelius, Oregon. President of our own logging and excavating company, Ron has shown me an out of doors side of life most women, and especially mothers these days, do not get the pleasure and pain of experiencing. Having been given my own small chainsaw with which to cut firewood from the scraps of broken trees as a sideline, I had the chance to build strength, get sore and sweat profusely. Then came the opportunity for a three- year stint as a part time file clerk and receptionist (what a difference!).

I wanted to do something to make a difference and a contribution. I wanted to create a book that anyone could relate to and enjoy, be made into an exciting movie without the abuse of profanity, violence or pornography that could still hold the reader's/viewer's attention and move them emotionally.

If nothing else I have enjoyed this time immensely, thank you to everyone who not only helped inspire this bit of effort, but who also had to put up with my mental absence this past year especially, and that would be my family. Thanks to my wonderful husband who watched as the house-work piled up, to my kids who wanted to play computer games but were told to "Go outside and play!" instead, because mom is on the computer, again.

Smiles, Carolyn Moor

JESSA'S PRAYER

Living in solitude in the Canadian wilderness, Jessa longs for the return of her husband. He is working in China as a geologist on a global team including seismologists and volcanologists, the only people on the planet able to detect and predict when, where and how hard an earthquake, eruption or tsunami will hit.

Grant has disappeared in a landslide and Jessa and Ian set out to find out what has happened. Together they find international government intrigue, technologies able to manipulate seismic activity, and even Mother Nature itself.

Battling snow- storms, flooding and fear itself, the two friends travel by horseback, motorcycles, and helicopter to name a few modes of travel enlisted.

Will she find him? Will he be alive? Ian finds himself wishing the latter of his missing friend as he falls in love with the man's wife.